--- ★ ---

At any other time of year the finding of a dinner-suited body on a beach might have had the touch of the surreal; last night, however, had been New Year's Eve and no doubt Winterton had been to a party of some sort.

Roper's gaze raked slowly up the fissured cliff face, looking for outcrops or shelves from which the body might have bounced like a soggy rubber ball to account for that twelve feet six; but there were none. If anything, at this part of the cove, the cliffs were dangerously undercut from top to bottom.

So murder it was. Or something very like it.

--- ★ ---

"[A] satisfying example of the classic British mystery..."

—*Booklist*

Previous titles from Worldwide Mystery by
ROY HART

A PRETTY PLACE FOR MURDER
A DEADLY SCHEDULE

Forthcoming from Worldwide Mystery by
ROY HART

A FOX IN THE NIGHT
ROBBED BLIND

Roy Hart

SEASCAPE
WITH
DEAD
FIGURES

WORLDWIDE.®

TORONTO • NEW YORK • LONDON
AMSTERDAM • PARIS • SYDNEY • HAMBURG
STOCKHOLM • ATHENS • TOKYO • MILAN
MADRID • WARSAW • BUDAPEST • AUCKLAND

SEASCAPE WITH DEAD FIGURES

A Worldwide Mystery/March 1998

First published by St. Martin's Press, Incorporated.
Reprinted by arrangement with Harold Ober Associates
Incorporated.

ISBN 0-373-26268-X

SEASCAPE
WITH
DEAD
FIGURES

ONE

THE TWO GULLS wheeled and swooped hopefully overhead, perhaps remembering the summer visitors who had tossed them scraps from their picnics, their memories triggered, maybe, by the small group of men engaged in slow but methodical activity at the foot of the cliffs. Few humans ever congregated at Monk's Cove in the depths of winter.

A foghorn throbbed faintly out at sea, although there was no sign of the ship that had sounded it. Closer to the land, the pulsing Xenon lamp of the Nun's Head buoy flashed in the greyness. It would snow soon.

With an unlit cheroot in his mouth, Roper stood with his back to the sea, his hands plunged deeply into the pockets of his sheepskin driving coat.

The body was cold, its clothes damp. Ergo: it had been lying down here on the shingle for several hours. The limbs were buckled like a badly treated rag-doll. Ergo: it had fallen from the cliff top. And, lastly, it was lying further from the base of the cliffs than it ought to have been. What little of Newtonian physics Roper knew could have been written on the back of a postage stamp; but what he did know was that a man could leap no further forward into fresh air than he could on hard ground. Ergo: the body, whether alive or dead, had been helped on its way down here. There was, therefore, a suspicion of mur-

der, or manslaughter, or, at best, the attempted dis-
posal of a body...

The foghorn throbbed again. The two gulls had
become four. They hovered warily half-way up the
limestone cliff face, from the top of which everyone,
Roper included, had initially presumed that Winterton had either fallen or jumped. A fall or jump of
some fifty feet. Fuzzily silhouetted high up against
the lead-grey sky, a police cadet was feeding down
a surveyor's tape to a constable on the beach so that
the guess would soon be verified. The same tape had
already been used to measure the shortest distance
from the body to the cliff face. It had turned out to
be twelve-feet-six. And that, in Roper's estimation,
was about six or seven feet further than a frail little
old man like Winterton could possibly have jumped.

The spot on the cliffs whence Winterton had
fallen—or whatever—was the centre of a geological
subsidence. To east and west, the great slabs of Port-
land limestone rose sharply to a couple of hundred
feet then formed the two spurs that made the horse-
shoe of the cove which then sloped down again out
to sea. On the eastern spur stood the old lighthouse
which the new buoy with its electronic gadgetry had
superseded; on the western the tea hut, shuttered and
closed for the winter.

Roper tossed his cheroot towards the incoming
sea and crunched back up the shingle, his every outward breath turning to vapour. Near the body, a flash
came from the camera wielded by the scene-of-
crime photographer, and up on the cliff top the
coastguards' Land Rover was parked and its crew
were setting up a winch to haul up the body when
Dr. Harford was finished with it. Further round the

cove two lines of raincoated and gumbooted constables were slowly advancing from opposite ends as they quartered the shingle.

Roper joined Miller on the other side of the body from where Harford knelt on a plastic sheet.

'Found anything else?'

Miller shook his head. The only find so far had been a walking stick. It had been lying a few yards from the body; although it might or might not have been Winterton's. It was, quite simply, a walking stick, a good solid hawthorn that could have been bought from any one of a half-dozen shops in the town. It presently depended from one of Miller's little fingers on a short length of string.

Then, as if in further answer, a distant shout came from one of the gumbooted uniformed men who had been scouring the shingle from the direction of Nun's Rock at the westernmost tip of the cove. He was holding high what appeared to be a hat.

'Tide's on the change,' observed Miller.

'I'd noticed,' said Roper. Another hour and the shingle here would be awash right up to the cliffs.

Dr. Harford's thumb experimentally closed Winterton's staring right eye. But as soon as he lifted his thumb the lid sprang open again.

'Already into rigor,' he commented, and the uniformed sergeant standing behind him and acting as the Coroner's Officer made a note.

Winterton lay on his back. He had not been a large man in life and death had further diminished him. The broken calf of his left leg lay under the thigh of his right with a kind of airy negligence. His pinched, lined face was bluely tinged, the mouth agape, the dentures askew in a last macabre leer.

Harford took up one of Winterton's hands from the shingle and finger by finger carefully tugged the glove from it. The fingers were stiffening, not quite into rigor, but almost. The back of the hand was flecked with the rustlike stains of old age, the fingernails immaculately clean and manicured.

The electronic-flash on the camera popped again and Harford's plastic-sheathed fingers loosened the body's Crombie overcoat and woollen muffler. Underneath, Winterton was in full evening fig, bowtie, stiff shirt, silk-lapelled dinner suit.

The cadet who had found the hat came breathlessly across the shingle and Roper turned away to join him. The wind was veering. It was coming off the land now, from the north. Radio Solent had forecast snow by the early evening, but Roper reckoned sooner, by lunchtime perhaps.

It was—or had been—a trilby hat of some quality. From Austin Reed's in London, according to the inscription on the silk label sewn into the crown. Size six and seven-eighths. Dark brown. But at the moment just a soggy, waterlogged mass of felt, with a sodden silk ribbon above the brim and a limp bedraggled feather sticking out of it.

'Where did you find it, son?'

As Roper got older so did the young get younger. This one was an uncut boy with pink cheeks, bright eyes and the strap of his cap lodged under his chin to stop the wind blowing it off. He pointed helpfully.

'About thirty metres this side of Nun's Rock, sir... That tall slab there. The one on the lean.'

'Nothing else, though?'

The lad shook his head apologetically. 'No, sir. Sorry. Only the hat.'

Roper passed back the dripping trilby.

'Take it to Inspector Miller, son.... And tell him exactly where you found it.'

The cadet threw up a salute with the kind of violence that would have done him credit on a parade ground and doubled away clumsily in his gumboots.

Roper trudged after him, drying his hands on a handkerchief. In the rush to get here he had forgotten his gloves. He had woken at a quarter to eight to the strident summons of the telephone. At five-to Miller had been waiting outside with the car and Roper had climbed into it still half-asleep, unshaven and still knotting his necktie. Awake now, though. Wide awake and the air going into his lungs like icy needles.

Winterton's body had been rolled over on to its face and was suffering the final indignity of having its trouser seams cut with a pair of surgical scissors to bare its buttocks.

Miller turned queasily aside as Roper came up beside him.

'Not the best way to start the year, is it?'

'It's good for our souls, laddie,' said Roper, hitching his muffler higher up his throat. 'Reminds us of our own bloody mortality.'

From the cliff top, the coastguards' aluminium-framed rescue stretcher was being winched down the rocks and one of the coastguards was abseiling down beside it.

Harford sank back on his hunkers while he waited for the rectal thermometer to register the body's internal temperature. A conventional thermometer lay on the top of his case beside him to record the ambient. It was fast creeping down to zero Celsius.

Roper gave a pluck to the knees of his trousers and crouched by Winterton's head. There was a definite depression at the crown of the skull and coagulated blood matting the milky-white hair about it. The blood appeared to have flowed forward, towards Winterton's ears, not downward to the nape of his neck; and there was blood on the stiff white collar of his shirt and the collar of his jacket—but none on the overcoat collar or the muffler.

'Take a shot of that, will you. Close as you can.'

Roper levered himself up and stood aside while the photographer crouched and focused for a close-up on the back of Winterton's head. The flash popped again.

'What do you make of that?' asked Roper.

Harford shuffled sideways and peered closely at the wound.

'No penetration to speak of.'

'The old blunt instrument? Or did he bang his head on the shingle?'

'Either—or both.... But I'd say he definitely came down feet first. Lot of damage to the legs and pelvis.... Spine feels reasonably intact.... A couple of cracked ribs.'

'What do you think he could have managed by way of a long jump?'

'You serious?'

'I'm always bloody serious,' said Roper.

'Well...I'd say he was a fit man for his age.... If he put his mind to it, say five, perhaps six feet.'

He shuffled back to where he had been beside Winterton's naked behind. He held aside the material of the trousers and underpants. Each wrinkled buttock was indented with the mesh-pattern of the underpants, as sharply defined as a newly minted coin, and here and there the more irregular blotches caused by the upward pressure of the shingle. These blotches were strikingly pale, and bordered with a distinct redness like the blush on a girl's cheek.

'Significant?' asked Roper.

'Possibly,' said Harford, peering up at Roper over the thick black rims of his spectacles. 'Hypostasis. Post-mortem lividity.... Gravity tends to draw the blood down—except where the pressure on the veins and arteries tends to inhibit the downward tendency—leaving those paler contact patches. Where the blood has been stopped off, as it were. They give a fair indication of how long the body's been lying here.... Six to seven hours, say.'

'Did he die here?... On the beach?'

'I couldn't say. More than likely, though.'

'Not much blood on the shingle,' said Roper. 'Hardly any, in fact.'

Harford made no comment. Daintily, fastidiously, he drew out the rectal thermometer. A barely audible whisper of gas escaped with it. Harford wiped the Vaseline from the thermometer with a tissue and tipped it towards the murky daylight.

'A shade below thirty-three degrees,' he said over his shoulder to the Coroner's Officer. Then to Roper: 'So he's been dead for about five hours—give or take a couple. Depends on a few more readings, of course. They'll be able to tell you more accurately when they've got him in the mortuary.'

Roper slid back a couple of layers of cuff to look at his watch.

It was five minutes to nine. So Winterton had died at some time between two and six that morning. At any other time of the year the finding of a dinner-suited body on a beach might have had a touch of the surreal; last night, however, had been New Year's Eve and no doubt Winterton had been to a party of some sort.

Roper's gaze raked slowly up the fissured cliff face, looking for outcrops or shelves from which the body might have bounced like a soggy rubber ball to account for that twelve-feet-six; but there was none. If anything, at this part of the cove, the cliffs were dangerously undercut from top to bottom.

So murder it was. Or something very like it.

THE LONG HAUL up the cliff path winded him, so that he had to stand for a few moments to get his breath back. It was even colder up here, the breeze stiffer. It was, or rather had been, his day off, and he had looked forward to spending most of it with a book and a bottle and his feet stretched out towards a blazing fire; an idea clearly disapproved of by whatever deity it was up there beyond the greyness who looked after the welfare of middle-aged policemen.

Winterton's body had beaten him up here. Shrouded in a zippered black plastic sack it was presently being slid into an ambulance. Down below the tide was coming in rapidly, and the area where the body had been found was being hastily marked out with iron stakes. Another hour and any evidence that might have been down there would be washed away altogether.

He walked on up the slope to where a tarmacadamed road ran due east to due west. A wire fence separated it from the grass and scree of the cliff top.

On the far side of the road, to Roper's left, stood the ruins of the old Cistercian priory. Sacked by Henry when he seceded from Rome, and finally reduced to its present state by Cromwellian roundshot, all that had withstood both was the bell-tower in the north-west corner. On this chill first morning of the new year it stood etched against the sky like a ragged exclamation mark.

Roper eased himself between the upper strands of the wire fence and crossed the road to the line of police vehicles drawn up on the other side. In the coach that had brought the posse of cadets from Dorchester, Saul Crossways sat uneasily, answering Miller's questions and demanding his bottle of moonshine back between times.

'I got rights, guv'nor,' he said, adopting a more wheedling tone in the face of higher authority, as Roper climbed into the coach. 'I came by that bottle honest.'

Roper held out his hand for the bottle and the constable who had temporarily impounded it passed it over. Roper unscrewed the cap and cautiously sniffed at the contents. He grimaced, and quickly stoppered it again.

'Smells like a cross between paint stripper and brake fluid. What is it, for God's sake?'

'Sherry,' said Crossways helpfully. 'And a little drop of meths to put some bite in it.... You can have a drop if you like, guv'nor. Keep the cold out.'

'No, thanks,' said Roper, sitting down on the seat across the aisle and handing the bottle back to the constable who was perched in the driving seat.

'I been half an hour without a sip, Mr. Miller,'

pleaded Crossways. 'A whole half-hour.... And you know how me chest is, don't you, Mr. Miller.'

Saul Crossways, vagrant and occasional police informer, was Redbury's stoically borne cross. Winter and summer he trailed about in the same threadbare overcoat and carried his plastic carrier bag of mysteries. The one presently between his knees had come from Woolworth's and was gaudy with a Yuletide illustration and the belated adjuration to have a merry Christmas. His enormous wealth of beard might kindly have been described as Mosaic, except that it was a matted grey tangle of hair and grease and sundry indications of what he might have eaten yesterday or perhaps even the day before that. His equally disordered hair sprouted from beneath his cap like a pair of badly-shorn wings. But blessedly he was as near sober as Miller had ever seen him.

'How did you come to find him?'

Crossways had been collecting wood, he explained. For his fire.

'Fire?'

'There.' Crossways jerked a woolly-mittened thumb towards the ruins just visible through the steamed-up windows. He had been camping there illicitly since the day before Christmas Eve, despite the many notices warning of the danger of falling masonry. He had made himself a temporary lair in the crypt under the bell-tower, venturing from it only when it was necessary to forage for food, alcohol and tobacco.

'...Don't like the town,' he said sulkily. 'Specially at Christmas. Brings out all the yobs and muggers. Frail old bloke like me—wouldn't be safe, would I, among all them 'obbledehoys?'

'You're kidding,' said Miller drily.

'No, serious, guv'nor,' protested Crossways, who was entirely without humour after half an hour without his tipple. 'Straight up. I nearly got me head beat in last Christmas twelvemonth. I reported it. Remember? So this year I stayed away. Kept m'self to m'self like.'

'What time did you go down to the beach this morning?'

'I don't know. Haven't got a watch, have I.... About half-six I suppose.'

'It was dark then.'

'I got a torch.' Crossways leaned forward and delved into his plastic carrier bag. From the clutter in it he produced a torch. It was brand new, rubber-coated, with a pristine, gleaming reflector. Roper suspected its provenance, but passed no comment. Crossways proudly worked the switch a couple of times.

'So you went down to the cove. Then what?'

'I started looking for bits of wood on the Nun's Head side. Then worked me way back to where I found him.'

'Did you touch him?'

'Never.' Crossways shuddered dramatically. 'I shone me torch—and he was staring straight at me.... And I recognised him, too, see.... He was the old bloke who lives up at that posh gaff—West-winds—you know? And he was a dead 'un all right. I shone me torch and he didn't blink. That's how I knew, see. Didn't have to touch him.'

'What then?'

Crossways screwed up his face while he tried to remember.

'Well,' he said. 'I come back up here. Dumped me few bits of wood in the doss, then I went along to tell the coastguards. Got there about half-past seven. They got a clock on the wall, see. They gave me a nice cup of tea; phoned your lot, then gave me a lift back here. And that's it, guv'nor. Honest.'

'How about during the night? Did you hear anything?'

'Like what?'

'A car stopping. Anything that sounded like a fight. Voices. Anything a bit out of the ordinary.'

Crossways shook his head.

'Not a dickey.'

Roper rose from his seat and buttoned his sheepskin.

'Show us this doss of yours, will you?'

With a hopeful but unrewarded glance towards his bottle, Crossways reluctantly got up and led the way from the coach and across the frosted grass to the ruins of the old priory, little more now than a rectangle of tumbled stone walls with just a hint of an arch where its entrance had once been. The flagstones that had been its floor had been removed long since and were doubtless serving the same purpose now in a local cottage or two. The only feature of note was the bell-tower, and it was towards that, with his grimy overcoat flapping about his ankles, that Crossways led them.

He picked his way cautiously down the ice-sheeted spiral of stone steps to the crypt and shone his torch about. Some four paces one way and five the other, the small damp chamber was rank with his habitation. It was floored with old and laminating tombstones, and here and there about the irregular walls was the glitter of frozen condensation. Roper took the torch and homed its beam into a corner where a stack of crushed cardboard cartons was serving as Crossways' bed. A single moth-eaten blanket lay crumpled at the bottom, a hessian sack stuffed with old rags at the top. Close to the bottom of the steps were the feathery grey ashes of a wood fire. Some kindling wood leaned against the wall nearby, some of it tinder-dry, some of it, obviously collected from the beach this morning, still dripping moisture into a spreading dark stain on the floor.

'And you're sure you didn't hear anything?' asked Roper. 'Nothing that might have sounded like a scrap of some sort?'

'Nothing,' said Crossways. 'It's like a grave down here.... Hark for yourself.'

Roper cocked an ear towards the stone arch at the foot of the steps. As Crossways had said, it was as still as a tomb down here.

Then, in the torchlit gloom, Crossways' rubbery, grizzled face took on a wily look of dawning.

'Here,' he said, shuffling closer and treating Roper to the full force of his numerous and indeterminate fragrances. 'Scrap?... Think he was done in do you, guv'nor, that old toff on the beach?'

Roper didn't reply, at least not in so many words.

'Now, listen,' he said. 'Watch out for yourself for the next few days, eh?.... Get yourself into the Sally Ann.... Take my point, do you?'

Crossways did indeed take the point, but perhaps not in the way Roper had in mind. His eyes glittered shrewdly as he took back his torch.

TWO

WINTERTON'S BODY had been driven off to the mortuary, and apart from Roper and Miller, and the two constables detailed to patrol the area and to keep any strollers at bay, the cliff top was desolate again.

Within a perimeter of fluorescent tape hung on iron stakes, Roper and Miller crouched and surveyed the spot from which the body had fallen—or whatever—at the middle of the geological depression that sloped back up to the road in front of the priory. A ragged path led from one to the other, little more than a scar of limestone and scree gouged out of the grass on either side. What little earth there was round about had been frozen as hard as cement for days. There was no sign of anything untoward having happened up here. No footprints, no scuffed grass, no signs of a struggle. No anything.

Roper stood up and went as close to the edge as he dared. From up here it looked an even higher drop than it had from the beach: 15.24 metres—according to the cadet who had measured it—or fifty feet, near enough, in imperial measure after he had applied himself, at Roper's request, to his pocket calculator.

Miller came up beside him.

Down on the beach, the iron skewers that marked where the body had been were already being licked by the tide.

'What do you know about aerodynamics, laddie?'

Miller shrugged. At twenty-eight already an inspector, he was one of the new breed of technocrat policemen, with a university degree under his belt and a chief superintendent's insignia ready and waiting in his raincoat pocket. He also objected to being anyone's laddie, although he didn't say so. This was his patch and his murder—albeit his first murder—and he objected to this iron-nosed brass-hat from the County Serious Crimes Squad stealing his thunder, as undoubtedly he would.

'Perhaps his overcoat acted like a parachute.'

'Wind was blowing the wrong way. From the south. It would have blown him towards the cliffs, wouldn't it? The coastguards say it started to change at about half-past seven. And that's about the time Crossways found him.'

They both leaned back against a sudden gust of wind that blustered down the slope behind them. If anything, the clouds were greyer and lower now than they had been half an hour ago.

'And supposing Crossways hadn't found him?' suggested Roper.

'He'd have floated out on the ebb,' said Miller. In which case the body might not have turned up for days, and then possibly miles from here, perhaps even in another county. Half-way out into the cove an abrupt shelf in the rocks set up a fierce undertow that made swimming here dangerous even in good weather. It would have sucked the body out for a mile or more.

Roper dropped to his heels again and took up a couple of pebbles. One he tossed out over the edge, the other he merely let fall. The first splashed into the sea close to the oval of stakes, the other completely out of sight at the foot of the cliffs. And Roper came finally to the indisputable conclusion that, if he had wanted to land among those stakes, he would have to have climbed back up the slope a few yards and then taken a running jump into space.

'He was thrown over, laddie,' he said grimly, along his shoulder to Miller. 'You can bet your bloody life on it.'

WINTERTON'S HOUSE stood against a background of winter-naked woodland on the western outskirts of the town.

A high wall of mellow bricks, crumbling here and there where a century of frost had attacked them, cut off the grounds from the road; and already Roper could smell money.

Miller drove in between the two ball-finialled brick columns of the gateway. The view of the house came and went between the trees. The odour of money grew stronger.

The house was Georgian, the genuine article, built in the days when the squirearchy around here was also the genuine article, an elegantly double-fronted box in a couple of acres of grassland and trees. Well away to the right of the house was a double garage—distinctly un-Georgian—but discreetly lost among a stand of chestnuts so that you had to look twice to see it.

Miller cut the engine and ratcheted on the handbrake in front of the white porch.

Cut-glass, thought Roper, sizing up the house again through the windscreen.

He ground out his cheroot in the ashtray and hitched up his muffler.

'Fit?'

Miller nodded and took out the ignition key and swung his feet out on to the tarmacadamed apron in front of the house.

In the window to the right of the porch stood an unlit Christmas tree. In the window on the left the curtains were still closed. The white window frames were all newly painted, the oak front door newly varnished.

A set of chimes carilloned from somewhere deep inside as Miller bowed a thumb against the bell-push and lifted it off again.

Roper braced himself. This part of the job was never easy.

He had been the bringer of bad news more times than he could possibly remember; all the kinds, from street accidents to the finding of a kid's mutilated body in a roadside ditch. He had never found a formula for doing it.

The door was opened. A woman. Tall. Slim. Dark.

'Yes?' The one word came with a crack like a pistol shot that seemed to ricochet around the porch.

'Good morning, madam.' Roper brandished his warrant card like a season ticket. She scarcely gave it a glance. About forty, sleek and stylish in a white shirt and tight black trousers. A glass of gin with a slice of lemon in it still in her hand. 'Detective Superintendent Roper, madam; County Police. And this is Detective Inspector Miller, Redbury C.I.D.'

She was not impressed. Above her elegantly sculpted nose a pair of sharp dark eyes flicked superciliously from Roper to Miller and back again.

'And what do you want exactly?'

'First of all, madam, who are you? Exactly,' asked Roper, as he tucked his card back under layers of sheepskin and muffler. 'Are you in charge here? Or what?'

'I happen to be Mr. Winterton's daughter-in-law,' she said curtly. 'And if you've come to see Mr. Winterton, you'll have to come back later. He isn't up yet. Sorry.'

Roper put his toe on the threshold because she looked the type who was likely to close the door in his face.

'I think it's your *husband* we need to see, madam.... If he's in.'

'What about?'

'Please, madam. We *would* like to come in if we may.'

There was a brief battle of wills. Roper won it, and she drew back a pace taking the edge of the door with her. Roper ushered Miller in front. The hall was oak-panelled up to waist height. A couple of dark seascapes in oils hung in gilt frames, one on either wall. A half-moon table beside the door looked like a piece of Sheraton, on it a telephone and a cut-glass ashtray.

'You'd better come in here.' She led them into the lounge, the room with the unlit Christmas tree in the window, then returned to the hall. Roper heard the telephone tinkle as she picked up the receiver. There was a strong sour smell in the room. Cigarette smoke and stale sweat. The after-odours of a party.

The lounge spanned the house from front to back. The electric chandeliers looked like adapted antiques, and the silver cigarette-casket on the brass and glass coffee table was either a late-Victorian

piece or a first class copy. Silver candlesticks on the
stone ledge above the fireplace, a dozen or so Christmas cards arranged between them and a brass-
framed carriage clock in the middle; and above that
a large rectangular mirror in an ornately baroque gilt
frame....

Roper broke off his stocktaking as the telephone
clattered back on to its rest in the hall.

Mrs. Winterton reappeared.

'Please sit down,' she said. 'And take off your
coats, if you wish. My husband's on his way over
now.'

'Thank you,' said Roper, and he and Miller
ranged themselves in the two chintz-clad armchairs
on either side of the fireplace. Both loosened their
outer coats and Roper unwound his muffler. The
room was hot. A newly-lit log fire spat in the grate;
on his way along the hall, Roper's hand had brushed
against a hot radiator. The Wintertons obviously had
a penchant for their creature comforts.

The inevitable silence followed, inevitable because to Roper this was a stock situation. He and
Miller were interlopers in a household that, until a
few minutes ago, had been jogging along evenly
with its day to day business. Now the police were
here, unheralded strangers who had still to say why
they had called, reticent, mysterious.

That shepherdess on the sideboard; a piece of
genuine Meissen, surely. A galleried silver tray beside it. No sign of an alarm system anywhere. A
housebreaker's delight and an insurance company's
nightmare.

The tension broke abruptly as a door slammed
and someone came into the house from the back. A

rush of water splashing into a metal sink, the rip of a paper kitchen towel; then a heavy footfall along the hall.

Roper and Miller both rose as Winterton's son turned into the lounge. Fortyish, grey curly hair, stockily built, that quick first impression also noting that the broad shoulders under a geometrically-patterned pullover were powerful enough to throw an elderly, lightweight man over a cliff without too much trouble.

'Apologies, gentlemen,' he said, glancing from one to the other of them. 'I've been changing a wheel on my bloody car.' A chill hand, still slightly damp, was proffered to Miller, then to Roper. It was a firm handshake, strong but controlled. He introduced himself as Julian Winterton.

'Now what's all this about?'

Roper backed to the armchair where he had been sitting. Miller did the same, and Winterton, following their lead, which Roper had hoped he would, lowered himself to the edge of the settee.

'We have some grave news for you, Mr. Winterton,' said Roper, after a moment or two spent looking down at his shoes. Then glancing up, as it were measuring Winterton's readiness, he went on:

'It's about your father…Mr. George Winterton. I'm afraid he's dead, sir.… I'm sorry.'

And that was it, finally slamming the door in the poor man's face. You could dress it up any way you liked, but in the end it was simply an honest reporting of what was simply a fact, delivered with a certain regret and the obligatory official platitude.

To begin with the Wintertons' reaction was one of disbelief. No gaping mouths, no widening of the eyes or looks of horror. They simply did not believe it.

'But that's crazy, Superintendent,' scoffed Winterton incredulously, shooting a look at Miller as if he expected Miller to scoff with him, 'the old chap's still upstairs in bed.'

But Miller's expression remained as impassive as Roper's, and Winterton, receiving no response from that direction, shot that same incredulous glance at his wife.

'Isn't he?'

'Yes,' she replied, frowning. 'He asked not to be called… And I didn't…. I'll go….'

'You'll be wasting your time, madam,' broke in Roper, quietly but firmly as she half turned towards the door. 'Your father-in-law isn't up there. Believe me.'

Then to Winterton, he said:

'Your father's body was found on the beach at Monk's Cove round about quarter past seven this morning…. No question that it *was* your father, sir; no question at all…. I'm deeply sorry.'

Another silence fell. Winterton's face had stiffened as disbelief at last began to give way to acceptance. His wife, less emotionally involved perhaps, had paled slightly and lowered herself to the arm of the settee beside him.

A flaming log rolled forward in the fireplace, flared, then subsided in a shower of sparks.

Winterton reached out and patted his wife's hand that lay on her lap.

'Get us a drink, duck, will you?' he said. His voice had a tremor in it now. 'How about you gentlemen?... No, of course, it isn't allowed, is it,' he added hastily. 'How about tea?... Coffee?'

Roper, to Miller's obvious disappointment, politely declined. Roper was in the mood for something wet and warm inside him too, but he had early on learned that it was never wise to break bread, even of the metaphorical kind, with anyone who was still a suspect. It was always best to keep on the outside, at least in the beginning.

At the sideboard, a long Jacobean slab of nearly-black oak, Mrs. Winterton busied herself with a couple of cut-crystal tumblers and a decanter from the galleried silver tray.

'You understand that I have to ask you both some questions, sir.'

Winterton was still passing from one emotional state to another. 'Yes,' he said. 'Yes, of course.... But how?... What the *hell* was he doing down at the cove?... And that early?... *That's* what I don't understand.... And did he have a heart attack? Or what?'

'We don't know the answers to any of those yet, sir.

'But you *must* know *something*.... You're here, aren't you?... I mean *you're* a superintendent and this chap's an inspector.... A couple of heavyweights. Right?'

The stopper clattered back into the decanter and Mrs. Winterton turned away from the sideboard with two tumblers, a whisky in one, her freshened gin in the other. She passed one down to her husband and resumed her seat on the arm of the settee beside him. She sipped at her drink, while her husband took down a good half of his at a single swallow, shuddered, then hunched forward with his elbows on his knees and the tumbler pressed between his hands. He stared into the fire.

'You still haven't answered,' he said.

'There is a possibility of foul play, sir,' said Roper.

For a second or two Roper was the centre of a perfectly static *tableau vivant.* Mrs. Winterton's glass stopped in mid-rise. Her husband's gaze locked on to Roper's. He said dazedly:

'Christ, you don't think he was murdered, surely?'

'It is a possibility, sir, yes.... I'm sorry.'

JULIAN WINTERTON and his wife had arrived here on Christmas Eve. Their home was in Highgate, north London. He was the senior partner in an advertising agency, his wife a sub-editor on one of the more upmarket women's magazines. There were no children.

'On good terms were you, sir? You and your father?'

From the expression on Winterton's face, obviously not.

'No,' he conceded reluctantly. 'In fact this is the first time that my wife and I have been down here in fifteen years or more. We didn't get on. Haven't for years.... But about a week before Christmas the old chap rang me at the office.... Sort of proffered the olive branch...you know? And he was getting on, and neither of us is getting any younger, and I thought, What the hell.... So we drove down.... Reasoned we could always drive back again if it all looked like becoming a disaster.'

'But it didn't?'

'No…. It all went surprisingly well.'

'Oh, come on, Julian,' Glenda Winterton broke in. 'We were simply in a state of armed neutrality. You said so yourself.'

He glanced up crossly at her.

'We were *all* testing the water. And things *were* getting better. He made the effort and so did we…. And he is…was…my father, for God's sake.'

No real love lost there either, thought Roper. The wife was a cool customer, perhaps even a cold one. Thus far not even the smallest sign of real affection had come from one of them towards the other. She had shown little grief and uttered not a single word of consolation, or even touched her husband in any way that might kindly be construed as a gesture of sympathetic understanding.

According to both of them, the dinner-party last night had been uneventful. After dinner, talk had drifted into local politics in which neither Julian nor his wife had any interest; George Winterton had been a prominent member of the town council.

Between the two of them, with an occasional hesitation, they managed to recall the guest list. Eleven people in all, including themselves and George Winterton. Mr. Vestry, headmaster of Redbury School, a boys' private boarding school on the eastern edge of town; Hugo Faulkner, who owned the *Redbury Argus,* the local newspaper, and his wife; Mr. Tasker, George Winterton's solicitor, and his wife; the Reverend O'Halloran, the vicar of nearby St. Philip's church; and, of course, Grace Fowler….

'Fowler?'

'My father-in-law's housekeeper,' said Glenda Winterton. 'Living in.'

She managed to give the 'living-in' a lot more nuance than it possibly deserved; but for the time being Roper let the innuendo pass.

'Is she here now, this housekeeper?'

'She drove along to Bournemouth early,' said Glenda Winterton. 'I think she was hoping to pick up a bargain or two in the New Year Sales.'

'When she comes back, I'd like her to contact us. Tell her that, will you. That's ten people; who was the eleventh?'

His name initially escaped them. Big, sullen man, with a beard. Owned a pottery down by the harbour. Jack…something-or-other…

'Coverley?' hazarded Miller. 'Jack Coverley?'

'Yes, that's the chap. Jack Coverley. A bit Left, I thought; not my father's sort at all.'

Across the hearth, Miller added Coverley's name to his list.

'Damn right,' said Glenda Winterton, tipping down the last of her gin. 'But he's Mrs. Fowler's boy-friend, isn't he? And he couldn't be left out, could he? Not in *those* circumstances.'

Another of those poisonous drips of malice aimed at the housekeeper. Roper again registered it, but again declined to rise to it.

Julian Winterton suddenly clicked a finger and thumb together, 'And there was that girl, too.'

'Girl, sir?'

An agency maid-cum-waitress. Hired for the evening by Mrs. Fowler. Neither knew her name, nor that of the agency; only Mrs. Fowler would know either. The girl had left, after clearing the dining table and washing up, soon after half-past ten. The Reverend O'Halloran had left soon after eleven. He had had a midnight service to conduct; the late shift, as he had humorously called it.

The rest of the guests had stayed to see in the New Year. Some tipsily, some not. George Winterton had plied his guests remorselessly but he had drunk little himself; a sherry or two before dinner, a glass of wine—perhaps two—during it, and a brandy with his cigar afterwards. The only drink Julian saw him take after that was the watered-down brandy with which he had toasted in the New Year with his remaining guests.

'What sort of *mood* was he in, sir, your father?'

Winterton shrugged.

'As ever,' he said. 'His usual jovial, sarcastic self. And sober—and hale.... So if you're thinking he might have committed suicide or something of that sort, I can tell you here and now that he wasn't the type. He got too much out of life, old as he was.'

'And exactly how old was he, sir?'

'Seventy-five...I think.... There's a family Bible in the study. If it's important, I'll look it up for you.'

About the order of the remaining guests' departures both Winterton and his wife were equally vague; except that both recalled the leaving of Vestry, the headmaster. His elderly car had refused to start and Julian Winterton, Faulkner and Coverley had had to give it a push start down the drive to get it under way. That had been at about quarter to one, give or take a few minutes either way.

'And who left the house last, sir? Can you remember?'

Winterton thought that it was Hugo Faulkner; his wife thought it had been Jack Coverley.

'But you can't be sure?'

Winterton shook his head. 'No. Sorry. I should think the best person to ask would be Grace Fowler.'

'Damn right,' said Glenda Winterton again, pithily, and looked as if she intended to hint at something else until a warning upward glance from her husband quelled her to silence.

'When all the guests had left, sir…I take it that there were then the four of you left in the house: your father, yourself and Mrs. Winterton here, and Mrs. Fowler the housekeeper.'

'Quite.'

'And can either of you suggest which of you might have been the last to see Mr. Winterton alive?'

'I suppose it had to be Mrs. Fowler,' said Winterton. 'Glenda went up to bed at about half-past one; I stayed up for about twenty minutes talking to my father…he was over there.' He nodded to where Miller was sitting. 'And when I finally went up to bed, Mrs. Fowler was still pottering about in the kitchen, boiling up some milk for my father's nightcap.'

'Mrs. Fowler saw to my father-in-law's every need, Superintendent,' Glenda Winterton broke in quietly, smiling sweetly. 'Not a sparrow falls around here, as the Good Book says, unless Grace Fowler wots of it. If you take my point.'

Roper stared woodenly back at her.

'Meaning what, madam?'

She hitched a dismissive shoulder.

'Exactly what I say,' she said. 'She had the old man around her little finger…. And you'd better believe it.'

THREE

JULIAN WINTERTON led the way into his father's study and quietly closed the door. Frowning concernedly, he said:

'You'll have to excuse my wife's caustic outpourings about Mrs. Fowler, Superintendent.... The truth is that they don't exactly hit it off together.... God knows why. Glenda's usually extraordinarily rational, and Mrs. Fowler's a bloody nice woman.... My father's right arm, you might say.' When he frowned his forehead puckered like a bloodhound's. A woman might have considered him an inordinately attractive man.

'Understood, sir,' said Roper, as if the outpourings were already forgotten, sweeping an eye slowly about the room. All was grist. Evidence, hearsay, a chance-heard conversation in a pub. Glenda Winterton's opinions of Mrs. Fowler might not have been logged in Miller's notebook but they had been duly noted all the same.

A black leather-topped mahogany desk stood four-square in the middle of the study with its back to the fireplace. A greenly upholstered captain's chair sat behind it. The desk top was tidy, a place for everything and everything in its place; a brass desk-tidy with pens and pencils sticking out of it, a glass inkstand, a blotter in a tooled-leather frame, a pair of filing trays, one red, one black, a gilt-edged diary for last year.

A glass-doored bookcase nearby held a decade of *Wisdens,* last year's *Whitaker's Almanack,* several volumes of *Who's Who* and a clutter of what looked like reference books on antiques. The Turner sunset on the wall facing the desk—that *had* to be a copy.

It was the rack of walking sticks by the window, however, that finally captured Roper's attention. It was Edwardian, a circular gadget of oak and brass. It revolved. It held some twenty sticks, ranging from a silver-mounted malacca to a bang-up-to-date shooting stick with a red leather saddle. A number of holes in the upper disc were still to be filled. Julian Winterton could not say if one particular stick was missing or not.

'It was a new one, sir.... A hawthorn.'

Winterton, still shaking his head, abruptly changed his mind at that. 'Yes,' he said. 'Yes.... The old chap *did* have one like that.... Grace Fowler gave it to him for Christmas. But I don't see it here, do you?'

'No, sir.'

The two sashed windows that looked towards the downs were both securely latched. The chill rushed in as Roper opened one and examined the outside sill for any obviously new marks in the fine dusk on the woodwork. There was none.

He drew the window down again and secured the catch.

'Is there any chance at all that your father might have gone for a walk this morning, sir?... After you and your wife had gone to bed?'

Winterton very much doubted it. '...So far as I was aware he was only waiting down here for his cup of chocolate. As soon as he'd drunk that he was going up to bed.'

'Did you hear him come upstairs?'

'No.'

'Mrs. Fowler? Did you hear her, perhaps?'

'No. Sorry. Both my father and Mrs. Fowler sleep at the back of the house; Glenda and I have been put up at the front.'

'But there's only the one staircase, surely, sir?'

'No.... Mrs. Fowler has her own set of stairs from the kitchen.... She has her own flat up there.... Self-contained.'

'I see, sir,' said Roper. A floor-board creaked in the room over the study. Miller was being shown around up there by Mrs. Winterton.

Roper moved in behind the desk and picked up the diary.

'May I, sir?... Please.'

'Of course.... Look wherever you like.... Do you mind?' Winterton flourished a gold cigarette-case.

'No, sir,' said Roper. 'It's your house after all.'

'I think it's more Mrs. Fowler's now,' said Winterton, wryly. He plucked a cigarette from the case, then snapped it shut. 'The old chap's Christmas present,' he said. 'All I'm going to get, most likely.... Sorry, how about you?' He flipped the case open again and held it out. The inside of the lid was hall-marked.

'No, sir, thanks all the same.'

So Julian had no expectations of his father's estate; and knew it. So that was one motive disposed of, at least.

Roper started at the middle of the diary and riffled his way forward through it. Winterton had been a

copious recorder. Almost each page was crammed
with a sloping, spiky hand, very sure of itself; probably George Winterton's own; occasionally, though,
there was a one-line entry in a more rounded, fem-
inine hand with flamboyant circles instead of dots
over the i's. These latter entries were all to record
appointments. Definitely a woman's handwriting,
and Roper scarcely needed now to ask the question.

'Did your father have a secretary, sir?'

'Not exactly.... I think Mrs. Fowler looked after
that side of things as well.'

At the back of the diary a few pages had been
printed to carry over into the current year.

An entry for this very morning.... H.M. 10.30.

'Do you know who H.M. might be, sir.... There's
an appointment here for ten-thirty today.'

Ten-thirty was only five minutes away. That was
the first appointment that George Winterton would
not keep. The second was for tomorrow, at half-past
eleven in the morning. That one was with Tasker
the solicitor. Tasker was the one guest at last night's
party whom Roper knew, mostly by way of their
mutual business in the County Court.

'H.M.?... No. No idea. As I've said before, Superintendent, I'm not exactly a regular visitor to
Westwinds House these days.'

Both the entry for H.M. and Tasker had been written by Winterton himself. The remaining pages of
the diary were empty.

'You were going to look up your father's age in
a Bible, sir.'

'Yes. So I was.'

It was in the glass-fronted bookcase, a leather-
bound Bible, scuffed with use and with the gilt let-

tering on its spine looking more like rust, brass-cornered and brass-clipped. It smelled musty.

One page of family entries, the last one, had been ripped out, and quite recently if the cleanness of the fibres around the tear were anything to go by.

'I don't think there's anything sinister about that, Superintendent.... He's been sixty for years, or so he says.... He was vain, you see.... He probably tore it out himself to stop anyone finding out for sure how old he actually was.'

'My old grandmother did the same, sir. As you say, there's probably nothing in it.'

The Bible was closed and the clasp snapped shut and it was returned to the bookcase. Footsteps down the stairs and along the hall to the lounge would be Miller's and Mrs. Winterton's.

Roper was ready to leave; but Julian made a long job of closing the bookcase doors and turning the key in the lock. When he turned away from it he was wearing his bloodhound's frown again. He stuffed one hand into a trouser pocket and made a fist about his keys, and for a few moments appeared to find something of absorbing interest on the carpet between his shoes. All the signs, Roper thought, of a man about to impart a confidence as soon as he could find the appropriate words.

Taking a slow pace to the desk, Winterton twisted out his cigarette in the glass ashtray with a lot more care than was strictly necessary. The muted ring of the telephone in the hall came through the door. Roper wondered if the caller might be H.M....

'I don't even think it's all that important,' said Winterton, at last, hesitantly. 'And God forbid that I should tell tales out of school. But...' A brisk tread crossed the hall, and the telephone abruptly stopped ringing. Winterton drew up his shoulders, still uneasy. 'I think…I only think, mind…that my father had a quarrel in here last night. Here in the study, I mean.'

At about half-past ten, soon after the agency waitress had gone home, Julian Winterton had gone from the lounge to the kitchen to top up the ice-bucket from the refrigerator. He had heard his father's voice from behind the closed door of the study. A voice now sharp and crisp and incisive; then a snapped response. Another man's voice with anger in it.

'Who was the other man?'

Winterton fidgeted uneasily. 'Look…I could be wrong, Superintendent.… I could be making a hell of a lot of trouble for somebody who isn't even remotely concerned in this dreadful business.'

'Who, sir?' Roper persisted obstinately. 'It could be important.'

'…It was the headmaster chap.… Vestry.'

Julian Winterton did not know what the argument had been about. It was none of his business, and after only the slightest hesitation he had continued on his way to the kitchen.

But he was absolutely sure it was Vestry's voice he had heard in curt response to his father's; not because he had recognised Vestry's voice but because on his way back from the kitchen he had seen Vestry storm out of the study and return to the lounge.

'He was pale, and shaking.… You know?… I poured him a stiff Scotch.'

'I'm surprised he didn't go home,' said Roper.

'I don't think he wanted a scene,' said Julian.

'Anyway, a few minutes afterwards the Taskers joined him and he seemed to jolly up again.'

'And how was your father after this row, sir?'

'Oh…just a little red in the face, that's all. But after a few minutes you'd never have guessed that anything untoward had happened.'

'Did you see Vestry and your father talking together afterwards?'

Winterton gave a vigorous shake of his head. 'They avoided each other for the rest of the evening.'

'And your father didn't mention it to you afterwards, I suppose. After everyone had gone home.'

'No. Not at all.'

A little more grist, then. It might turn out in the end to be only chaff, to be blown away in the first real puffs of evidential wind, but for the time being it was worth dropping into the granary. The start of any investigation was always the lean time, and there was always the chance that it might yet get leaner.

Roper led the way out.

The hallway smelled of beeswax; just inside the front door the telephone on the half-moon table was back on its rest. Miller's voice came from the lounge. Both he and Glenda Winterton rose as Roper came in with Winterton behind him. Glenda Winterton had another tumbler of gin in her hand.

'Who was on the 'phone?' asked Winterton casually.

'Oh…that funny little man…Vestry,' said Glenda Winterton, with an airy flap of her hand. 'He wanted to speak to your father. I told him he was out.'

'And what did he say, madam?' asked Roper.

She shrugged. 'Damn... That's all. Then the line went dead.'

'...AND I'LL WANT AN OFFICE. And somewhere we can set up a murder room.'

'Incident room,' said Miller, correctly, but unwisely. He had hoped that the superintendent from County might only have come down on a flying visit to get the investigation under way. It seemed that he was going to stay.

'Murder room, son,' said Roper. 'Murder's no bloody incident. Right?'

And he wanted a sketch map—and the photographs from the beach—and a couple of dog-handlers—with two *good* dogs. Give 'em a sniff of Winterton's shoes when they come back from the mortuary and get 'em to sniff along that path from the road to the cliff edge. And.... And.... There seemed no end to the ands.

'We don't have two dog-handlers,' said Miller, correctly, but again unwisely.

'Then get on to County, son. Get on to County. Just get it done. Right?'

The cold trailed after them as they hurried in from the street. At the desk, a virago of a woman in a moth-eaten fur coat and with a squirming pekingese trapped under one arm was making a shrill complaint to the duty sergeant. The plump, seedy-looking man sitting on the bench under the window looked as if he was next in line after the woman with the dog, but he rose with a smug smile as he caught sight of Miller and moved to bar his way.

'If the circumstances were more meet, Mr. Miller,' he said. 'I'd wish you a Happy New Year.'

'And what makes you think they're not?' retorted Miller tetchily, skirting him on one side as Roper skirted him on the other. They reached the stairs.

'Hear you've got a murder on your hands, old chum,' he called after them. 'Is that right?'

Miller walked on up. Roper stopped and came back down again. Then Miller stopped.

'And just who are you?' asked Roper.

'Haggerty,' said the man, his dewlapped boozy face still with the smile plastered on it. He produced a card from deep inside his overcoat. '*Redbury Argus*—for my sins.... And I've seen *you* in court.... Superintendent Roper?... Serious Crimes?'

'And you've got a direct transfusion from the local grapevine—or what?'

'I had a 'phone call,' said Haggerty. 'Anonymous. Murder, it said.'

Roper glanced pointedly at his wristwatch. 'Inspector Miller's going to be busy, Mr. Haggerty. You can come up and talk to me. Five minutes.'

Miller showed them into his own cramped office and went off on the numerous errands that Roper had given him.

Roper hung up his sheepskin and muffler on the hook behind the door. Haggerty had already made himself comfortable in the visitors' chair and taken out his notebook.

'Now, Mr. Haggerty. Who told you?'

'I've told you already,' said Haggerty. 'A little bird. He 'phoned the rag from a public callbox—and asked me to reverse the charges. Claimed to have found a body on the beach earlier on. He reckoned you people suspected foul play. Old George Winterton, so he said.'

'Anonymous?'

Haggerty sketched a shrug with the hand that held his pencil. He was one of those unfortunates who, however they are turned out, always look slightly bedraggled and slightly unwholesome. His droopy-lidded eyes were still red-rimmed from his celebrations last night and a forelock of his thinning hair hung untidily above one eyebrow.

'That's what the man said. He called from a public box. Said if the rag cared to drop him a tenner, he'd got a headline for us. And eager old journalist that I am, I let him persuade me.'

'Any idea who he was?'

'Didn't ask. Never do. I agreed to drop the cash this afternoon, and he spilled the beans.'

'Where will you drop the cash?'

'Ah, well, very *Boy's Own*, that. Our Mr. Anon told me to leave the cash—in coins—under a stone beside the entrance to the old priory.'

Roper wearily crabbed a hand for Miller's jotter and scribbled a brief note to himself. Crossways was a garrulous old fool, but if murder had indeed been done down at the cove this morning then Crossways at large was clearly Crossways at risk.

Haggerty sprawled back comfortably in his chair. 'So what *are* you prepared to tell me?'

It was little beyond the events that had begun with the assistant chief constable's telephone call early this morning and ended with Winterton's corpse being winched up the cliffs to the coastguards' Land Rover. The approximate time the body had been found. The approximate time of death. The height through which the body had fallen and, with the assistance of a few pencilled lines on a scrap of paper, the exact spot on the beach where the body had been found.

Haggerty made a few notes, drew a sketch map.

'You still haven't answered the sixty-four dollar one.'

'I can't,' said Roper. 'I can't tell you because I don't know. He might have fallen or he might have been pushed. It's too early to say yet.'

'But what do you think? Off the record.'

'I've already answered that one: no comment.'

From somewhere in the folds of his overcoat Haggerty fished out a crumpled packet of Capstan Full Strength and a box of Swan Vestas. He sorted out the least bent cigarette and lit it. He inhaled greedily, held the smoke, then let it seep slowly out again. Then he said:

'How did Mrs. Fowler take it?'

Roper glanced across at him, surprised. 'You know Mrs. Fowler?'

Haggerty sagely tapped the wing of his broad, finely-veined nose. 'Eyes and ears of the world. That's me. What your people don't know about this town, yours truly does. Between the two of us we don't miss a trick, do we?'

Roper sighed.

'Don't mess me about, Mr. Haggerty. I don't have the time. Another couple of hours and I'll have the C.C. on my back as well. If you know something pertinent, then I want to know as well.'

'Oh, it's pertinent all right,' said Haggerty. 'At least, it's pertinent to Mrs. Fowler.' He drew on his cigarette and expansively exhaled a horizontal column of smoke. 'But if Mrs. Fowler isn't involved in old George's death,' he said quietly, 'you and I keep this between ourselves. Can you do that?'

'I don't know,' said Roper. 'Try it on for size and we'll see, shall we?' He dipped into his jacket for cheroots and lighter.

'I'm not suggesting that she did Winterton in, of course,' ventured Haggerty cautiously. 'But if she did, it won't be the first time she's been accused of something very like it.'

'Very like what?' asked Roper, now with a cheroot in his mouth.

'Murder,' said Haggerty.

Roper struck his lighter. Few things these days had the power to surprise him any more.

'Go on,' he said. 'I'm all ears.'

HAGGERTY HAD SEEN better days. In the late 'fifties he had been the chief crime reporter on one of the big London dailies.

He had covered the case in the summer of 'fifty-nine, at the Old Bailey, when a certain Grace Dacre had been arraigned on the charge of murdering one Gerald Fanning.

Both names struck a chord in Roper's memory, but only as distantly remembered headlines in old newspapers. Fanning had been an M.P., Dacre his children's nanny.

'She pleaded self-defence,' recalled Haggerty. 'Told the tale he'd come home boozed from a late night sitting and tried to rape her. She got him with a pair of scissors in the neck. Hit his carotid. Nasty.'

There had been no witnesses, nobody else in the house but the two children, and they had been upstairs in bed. Fanning's wife was in Paris at the time; with a racing driver boy-friend.

'But she got off,' said Roper. 'Didn't she?'

'Yes. Just,' said Haggerty. 'But only just. Fanning had been with her before, you see, on a regular basis. Jury thought that was very dodgy. And we hadn't hit the swinging 'sixties then; different social *mores,* and all that claptrap. So far as the jury was concerned, she cried rape a year or so too late. And there were two or three shaky bits of evidence, too. According to the elder daughter, when she came downstairs to see what all the racket was about, Miss Dacre was *au naturel.* Not a stitch of her glad-rags anywhere in sight.

'But there was a nightdress behind the settee—at least by the time the police arrived. It was covered in blood. Fanning's, of course. She swore she'd taken it off and flung it there; hysteria, perhaps. But the daughter insisted it wasn't there when she'd first come in. But Dacre's defence lawyer pleaded hysteria on the daughter's part as well. How would a child of ten see anything in detail with her father's bleeding body draped all over the hearth?'

And Grace Dacre had been little more than a child herself, young, pretty and plausible. After two hours out the predominantly male jury had returned with a verdict of not guilty. The case had then died, and Grace Fowler had dropped from sight.

'How did you get on to her down here?'

'Covered a Rotary Club dinner,' said Haggerty. 'About five years ago. Winterton was the guest of honour. The text of his speech was law and order—as ever. It was pretty inflammatory stuff, and to be fair to the man it was a bloody good speech, certainly fiery enough to make good copy.' Haggerty paused to light another bedraggled Capstan from the stub of another. 'I decided to interview him—he used to like to see his name in the rag—but I couldn't get near him until the dinner was over and everyone was leaving.... And there we were, deedily chatting away in a corner, when in comes Mrs. Fowler. She'd come to collect him in the car. The upshot was he introduced us. Said she was his housekeeper and general factotum, but I got the distinct impression that she was a hell of a sight more than that, if you see what I mean. When she helped him on with his coat, he said: "Thank you, Grace." And click! I made the connection.'

'A pretty tenuous connection, though, eh, Mr. Haggerty?'

'I was already half-way there,' said Haggerty. 'Her face had already struck a chord the moment I clapped eyes on her. And remember, back at the Bailey, I'd been watching her sitting in that dock every day for nearly a fortnight. Part of our stock-in-trade, faces are. We don't forget 'em, especially in those circumstances.'

'And just how sure are you?'

'Ninety-nine per cent,' said Haggerty. 'Take my word for it; Grace Fowler and Grace Dacre are one and the same lady.'

FOUR

IT WAS HALF-PAST ELEVEN. Haggerty had gone, and the side table in Roper's temporary office looked like a stall at a church bazaar. Winterton's effects had arrived from the mortuary.

Polythene-bagged, they littered the table. There was nothing extraordinary among them; no more than there would be considering that their late owner had spent most of last night at his own dinner party in his own house. The only oddity was a pair of keys. One for a Yale lock and one for a Chubb mortice lock. On a ring. They raised a doubt.

Had they been found in Winterton's overcoat pocket, it might have been reasonable to suppose that Winterton had left them there unthinkingly after his last outing. But according to the typed list from the Coroner's Officer they had been found in the pocket of the dinner jacket. And what man walks about with his front-door keys in his dinner jacket in his own house? So perhaps, after all, Winterton had gone out last night after drinking that nightcap. Where? Why?

Too many questions; too few answers.

The only other loose items were the display-handkerchief—from the breast pocket of the dinner jacket—and Winterton's gold-cased Longines wristwatch.

The watch, with a single crack across its cover glass, had stopped at half-past five.

Tailor's tabs in the dinner jacket and silk-piped trousers showed that both had been made for Winterton in Bournemouth fairly recently, although the style and cut were ten years or so out of date. The starched shirt, bowtie, black silk socks and black shoes had made up the rest of his outer attire. His underclothes were more plebian. The labels were from Marks and Spencer. The still-damp urine stain on the front of the underpants might be indicative of a last moment of sheer blinding terror; or simply an old man's worn-out bladder letting him down in the cold of a winter's night.

The Crombie overcoat had been recently dry-cleaned; stapled to the lining of the ticket pocket was still a fragment of the cleaner's yellow label.

Roper thoughtfully picked them all over, looking for something, anything.

By their raiment shall ye know them; and from the anomalies of that raiment might ye even gain an inspiration or two: Julian Winterton had last seen his father at ten minutes to two this morning. In these clothes. Ergo: Winterton had not been to bed afterwards. Because a man summoned from it in the middle of the night might slip into a dinner suit if it was the first thing to hand, but he would never struggle into a bowtie.

Ergo: if Winterton had slept at all last night, it had been in his clothes.

The black shoes were strictly lightweight. Well worn but well kept. Polished to a sheen. The backs of the heels slightly scarred—but not a lot. Perhaps where they had hit the shingle. But definitely not the shoes for a long hike on a winter's night. The wafer-thin soles were polished from indoor use, scarcely a scratch on them.

Ergo: however George Winterton had got to Monk's Cove from Westwinds House last night, he certainly had not walked there.

Two small, tear-shaped, bloodstains on the stark white of the stiff shirt collar were more or less matched by two dark-brown spots on the collar of the jacket. Neither muffler nor overcoat bore similar marks. The forensic lab might find otherwise, but if it did not then the conclusion had to be that both the overcoat and muffler—and hat—and gloves—had been put on Winterton *after* he had received that blow to the head.

Ergo: it was very unlikely that Winterton had gone to Monk's Cove this morning under his own steam. And it followed from that that Roper's guess that he might even have died somewhere else was not so very wide of the mark.

The hawthorn walking stick still had Miller's loop of string around its hooked handle so as not to smudge any latent prints. To the naked eye it looked unmarked.

Another mute witness?

Or the murder weapon?

In either case it had been lying on the shingle this morning within a yard or two of Winterton's body. Ergo: it was material evidence of some sort or another. Like the Longines wristwatch that had stopped at half-past five.

JUST BEFORE MID-DAY the first of the snow began to fall, heavy, swirling flakes that were already settling on the pavements like a thick white dust.

The traffic lights changed to green and Roper eased the blue Ford into the Mall. The Mall was Redbury's axis, slicing the town in half from north to south. At its northern end it opened up to left and right around the Town Hall and the public gardens and the obligatory statue of Queen Victoria gazing towards the distant seafront, as it had for most of the last hundred years, with plump-cheeked disapproval. At the southern end it was given over to antique and gift shops and fish-and-chip parlours, an amusement arcade or two and a couple of bookmakers' shops. To the west of the Mall, old Redbury still lay curled up in the quietude of its Georgian and Victorian gentility. To the east, it was a product of the nineteen-twenties and 'thirties, gaudier, and noisier, and geared for the fleeting few months of the Season.

Roper pulled into the kerb behind Tasker's Citroën. On the first floor above Barclay's bank a light shone in one of the solicitors' office windows.

Gregory Tasker was somewhere in his middle sixties, a small bright gnome of a man with a neat Vandyke beard and a pair of quick shrewd eyes behind a pair of gilt-framed half-moon spectacles. His bluely tinged nose showed that he had not been here long himself.

His office was chilly and he was still in his overcoat.

'I appreciate your turning out, Mr. Tasker,' said Roper, as they shook hands.

'I still can't believe it,' said Tasker. 'You said murder.'

'I only said that I *thought* it was, Mr. Tasker.'

'Yes,' said Tasker crisply, as they loosed hands.

'But you and I know each other, don't we, Superintendent.' A brief gesture took in the visitors' chair on the opposite side of the desk from his own. While Roper sat down and loosened his sheepskin, Tasker went across to a bubbling percolator standing on a filing cabinet by the door. He returned with two Pyrex cups brimming with coffee that was as black as night and as sweet as treacle. He set one down in front of Roper and one on his own side of the desk.

'Right,' he said. 'How can I help?'

'I'm told you spent last evening up at Westwinds House, Mr. Tasker.'

Tasker nodded. 'Yes. My wife and I saw in the New Year there.' He hoisted the skirt of his overcoat and sat down in his swivel chair and stirred his coffee.

'Mr. Winterton acting normally, was he?'

'Oh, yes,' said Tasker. He picked up his cup and took a slow meditative sip from it. 'He was in his usual form. Bustling—articulate—not a care in the world, I'd have said.'

'And sober when you left him?'

'Yes, indeed,' said Tasker. 'I can honestly say that I saw him drink very little all evening.'

So far as he could remember, Tasker and his wife had left Winterton's house just after five to one. He recalled Faulkner, Coverley and Julian Winterton pushing Vestry's car down the drive to get it started. To the best of his memory, that had been at about a quarter to one. As he had started his own car, he had seen Coverley climbing into his. They had called good night to each other.

'And that would have made Mr. Faulkner the last guest to leave, wouldn't it?'

'Yes. I'd say it would have.'

He repeated more or less what Julian and Glenda Winterton had told Roper about the dinner party. A quiet evening. Good food, good wine, congenial company. Although soon after dinner he *had* noticed a sudden hostile chill develop between Winterton and Clive Vestry. Tasker had no idea what had caused it.

'Vestry came back into the lounge—from some-where—white as a sheet and shaking—I mean *really* shaking. I thought the poor man was ill. I went across to see if he was all right. He told me it was nothing—a touch of nervous indigestion—and thought that he might go home. Then, while we were still talking, young Winterton came across with a stiff whisky for Vestry—I don't know whether Vestry had asked him for it or not but, anyway, Vestry took it, drank it, and then seemed to recover. But then I noticed that he and Winterton more or less kept their backs to each other for the rest of the evening. Rather childish, I thought, because it looked so very obvious. Would you care for an-other?'

'No, sir, thank you.' Roper set his cup back on its saucer. 'Do you mind telling me if you and Mr. Winterton were *close* friends? Or more business ac-quaintances.'

'A little of both, I'd say,' said Tasker. 'But if you want an honest answer, I would have to say that we were more business acquaintances. He was a client whose affairs I looked after personally. A rather im-portant one, I hasten to add. And one who always settled his bills on time.' Tasker's empty cup clinked back on its saucer and he dabbed a fastidious finger along the underside of his moustache.

'And a wealthy man—was he?'

'Yes,' agreed Tasker. 'But only comparatively speaking. He certainly wasn't a millionaire—or anywhere near to being one. But he certainly wasn't short of the odd shilling or two.'

'How about the state of his financial affairs?' said Roper. 'Sound, were they?'

'Remarkably so,' said Tasker. 'Most of his investments were here in the town. He had a small stake in the *Argus*, another in Coverley's pottery; that sort of thing, you know? Nothing large, nothing grand. He certainly wasn't a speculator. His interest lay more in propping up small local businesses to save them from going under. In fact, one could almost say that he was a local benefactor. He'd put several firms back on their feet—to his own advantage as well, of course—and as you know, he was a leading light on the town council, and on the parish council at St. Philip's church, and a member of the board of governors over at the Redbury Boys' School, and so on. On the whole, a most active and conscientious citizen.'

Roper savoured all this praise with his usual wariness, too old and experienced a dog not to know that there is no such thing as a blameless man—or woman, for that matter. He was as cautious of the human race *per se* as he was of stray dogs. Both were equally capable of wagging one end while contemplating a bite with the other.

'This interest Mr. Winterton had in the *Argus:* did he have that before the fire, or afterwards?' When the old *Argus* printing works had burned down a year or so ago, the County Fire Officer had thought he had smelled a whiff of arson, although a thorough investigation afterwards had drawn no conclusion either one way or the other. The files on the case were now stored at County, but by no means were they closed. Perhaps it was a time to draw them out and dust them down again.

'Afterwards,' said Tasker. 'It's all on public record. The insurance company were extremely tardy in paying out and Hugo Faulkner, poor man, very nearly went to the wall. George Winterton advanced him a substantial loan, of which Faulkner subsequently paid back half and gave Winterton a shareholding in the *Argus* to make up the balance. All copper-bottomed and above board, I assure you.'

Roper made a slight change of course.

'And how about his housekeeper—this Mrs. Fowler? What do you think Mr. Winterton's relationship was with her?'

'Oh, a marvellous woman,' Tasker replied enthusiastically. 'They got on extremely well together. She wasn't only his housekeeper, you know; she was also his secretary, chauffeuse, nurse and Heaven knows *what* else. A most remarkable woman. Truly remarkable...'

Then Tasker suddenly checked his enthusiasm in case Roper might have misunderstood.

'Not, I hasten to add, that there was *ever* a breath of scandal about the two of them. But they were, I know, very close. And I dare to say that she was the best thing that had happened to Winterton in years. That's only an opinion, of course. But I'm sure that anyone who knew the two of them will tell you the same.'

Roper wondered if Coverley would; Coverley who, according to Glenda Winterton's icily delivered asides, was Mrs. Fowler's man-friend, and perhaps even more than that.

And that thought led to another. Roper said: 'How about the beneficiaries of Mr. Winterton's estate?'

For a second or two Tasker's face seemed to close in on itself while he debated with himself where his professional loyalties lay.

'I'm really only prepared to show you the will against a magistrate's warrant,' he said. 'But, broadly speaking, the house and Winterton's business interests go to Mrs. Fowler; the more liquid assets go to the son, Julian. There are some other small bequests, to the school and so on, but they're only token. A few hundred pounds here and there, certainly no more.'

Roper felt the small, involuntary, fleeting together of his eyebrows as he recalled Julian Winterton's wry remarks this morning: 'I think it's more Mrs. Fowler's house now.' Then, as he had snapped shut his new, gold cigarette-case: 'All I'm going to get, most likely…'

It seemed that Julian had grossly under-estimated his expectations. Or had he?

'Did Mr. Winterton make any changes to his will, Mr. Tasker; in the last few months, say?'

'Why, yes. As a matter of fact he did. A week or so before Christmas.'

'How, sir?' And when Tasker again seemed unwilling to answer: 'It could be important, Mr. Tasker. A broad outline, that's all.'

Tasker gave an upward nudge to his spectacles. 'Well…' he began reluctantly. 'Broadly…since you ask...before the change, Julian didn't figure in the will at all. In fact...more than that...there was an exclusion clause, absolutely watertight in law, specifically stating that he should have absolutely nothing from his father's estate, and further stating, quite clearly, the reason for this exclusion. Julian could *never* have hoped to contest it.'

Roper could almost feel the water he was presently treading getting deeper, and thicker, and murkier. 'You know,' he said. 'I'd give my eye-teeth to know what was in that exclusion clause, Mr. Tasker.'

'As motive? Yes, I'm sure you would, Superintendent, but if I told you I would probably lay myself wide-open to a charge of malicious slander on the part of Julian Winterton.' Tasker smiled puckishly and the frames of his spectacles glinted in the light from his desk lamp. 'Which information you can either take as a strong hint, if you follow me, or forget in its entirety. Or perhaps you might ask Julian Winterton—and perhaps he might even tell you.'

'I'll take the option on the strong hint, Mr. Tasker. Thanks.' But whatever rift had stretched between Julian Winterton and his father, it had obviously been filled in by one or the other of them in the weeks preceding Christmas.

'He had an appointment with you tomorrow. Eleven-thirty. Do you know what he wanted?'

'Yes. His will. He intended to change it.'

'Again?'

'Yes. Again.'

'How? Did he say?'

'No, he didn't. He bearded me last night, a few

minutes into the New Year, hauled me out to his hall and insisted that he saw me this afternoon. It was a matter of some urgency, so he said. But I explained that I couldn't possibly do that; my daughter and son-in-law are driving down from Bristol to have lunch with us. So we arranged an appointment for tomorrow—much against Winterton's wishes. He really was most insistent.'

'Was he angry?'

Tasker considered for a moment, gave another nudge to his spectacles.

'Angry? No, not exactly. But certainly upset. I could be wrong, of course.' He spread his hands apologetically. 'All I know, Superintendent. But if I can help any more I shall be glad to.'

'Right, sir. Thank you.' Roper stood up and lifted his chair back a few inches to where it had been.

They shook hands again on the landing of the stairs that led to the street. Roper started down them, but only for two or three steps before he stopped and turned as one last question came to mind that Tasker might be able to answer.

'He had an appointment this morning, too. With an H.M. Do you know who that might have been, Mr. Tasker?'

Tasker gave it some thought, frowning. 'No, Superintendent,' he said at last. 'Sorry. I don't.'

Out in the Mall the snow was still tumbling down relentlessly and the Town Hall clock struck its single dolorous chime for half-past twelve.

FIVE

WITH A QUICK deft movement, like a conjurer revealing yet another rabbit, the mortuary attendant flicked down the shroud and exposed George Winterton's dead waxen face.

Julian Winterton's glance at it was only of the briefest kind. 'Yes,' he said, averting his face. 'That is my father.'

The eyes were closed now and the dentures properly in place. On the face was neither surprise nor pain, only a doll-like calmness.

'All right, chief?' asked the attendant, of Roper. He was a short, squat, unprepossessing young man, with broken teeth and hair cropped so short that his scalp showed through the stubble like a gleaming pink balloon. His left forearm was heavily tattooed with a memorial to his mother, his right with an elaborately detailed eagle. His constant dalliances with death in all its forms had bequeathed him a lugubrious cheeriness.

'Yes, son,' said Roper. 'Thanks.'

The attendant covered the face again with a showy delicacy. He might have been a butcher who took especial pride in the manner in which he parcelled up his meat. He slid the trolley back into the refrigerated cabinet and swung the door shut.

'Do you want me any more?' asked Winterton. 'Or can I wait outside?'

'Outside, if you like, sir.' Winterton was visibly

disturbed. He looked as if he might even be sick. 'Be with you in a couple of minutes.'

Winterton hurried out to the tiled passage, already patting around his pockets for his cigarette-case.

The attendant was a keen connoisseur of the wares that passed through his premises, a shrewd expert, much as the devoted collector of old paintings and antique furniture eventually becomes an expert.

'I got all his clobber off and laid him out, didn't I? Checked his internal temperature and had a good feel about. A fall. From a great height, as they say.' He bared his colourful battered teeth in a mirthless smile. 'Fifty...sixty feet. Anything much more than that and the old insides burst. Like a paper bag full of water. But he was a lightweight, and bundled up in that overcoat, it sort of protected him, like. Cushioned the fall...and it might have slowed him down a bit in the air. And he fell feet first—or he turned over in the air.' With an eloquent gesture the attendant described an arc with his right hand, lifting it high and swooping it down and revolving it. Then balled it into a fist and smote the palm of his opened left hand with it. 'Splat! Like that. Tell by the legs.'

Bones, he explained, got like old dry twigs at that age. Both of Winterton's legs had suffered multiple fractures, the right one shortened several inches by the impact.

And, like Dr. Harford, he had observed the mottled pink and white pattern on Winterton's buttocks.

'Hypostasis,' he explained. 'Hypostasis we call that. Means he was lying on the beach for a long time before he was found. Right, chief?'

'How long?'

The youth rolled his eyes upward while he considered. 'It'll be a guess, like. But about five or six hours.'

'You can't get closer?'

'No, chief. Sorry.'

And, probing, he had found at least two snapped ribs—true ribs. '—High up. Just here.' The young man turned his own broad muscular back and gave himself a half-nelson to demonstrate the exact site of the fractures. 'And a broken scapula—that's what we call the shoulder-blade. Right side, top to bottom.'

He turned back again. He smelled of antiseptic and formaline and the various other unguents of his trade. 'And when I put his body weight and temperatures in the old computer, the print-out said he died about half-past two this morning. But,' he added darkly sidling closer and glancing over his shoulder towards the door, 'that's allowing for the fact that he died outdoors. Eh, chief? Get me? Where you found him like.'

'And supposing he'd died indoors?'

'Ah, well that's different.' The attendant pursed his lips for a moment and contemplated the ceiling. 'Depends on how long he was dead before he was taken outside. You might have to take an hour off. Or at least a half.'

'And what about that wound at the back of his head?'

'Difficult to say, that one is, chief. Something flat, I reckon. A chunk of timber, something of that sort. I'm not an expert, mind,' he cautioned modestly. 'But there isn't any what we call penetration. Now, with an iron bar—or a spanner—or a wheel-jack

handle—something really hefty—with a small surface area—you get penetration. The weight of the
metal carries it on through the skull a bit—like a
knife in a slab of butter. But whatever hit *that* old
bloke was flat. Cracked his skull like an eggshell.
And maybe it didn't kill him, not at once anyway.
It could have just K.O.d him. In fact, it could be,
just could be, mind, that if he'd been got here to the
infirmary double-quick he might still be breathing.'

'There was blood in his hair,' said Roper drawing
a line from the top of his right ear to his temple with
the tip of his thumb. 'Means he was lying face down
for a while afterwards, right?'

The attendant's eyes brightened with admiration.

'Dead right, chief. Spot on. I noticed that
m'self—and something else, chief: there wasn't any
blood on the collar of his overcoat.' Clearly, as
Roper had seen fit to trespass upon his terrain, so
the attendant saw fit to trespass upon Roper's. 'An
hypothesis, okay? Somebody clobbered the old
bloke—but not where you found him. Somewhere
else. Could have been a burglar or somebody. Perhaps it was even in the old bloke's own place. Burglar gets the wind up. Gets the old man togged up
in his overcoat, carts him down to the cove and
dumps him over the edge to make it look like an
accident—or a suicide. There were *three* suicides
down there last year, so nobody would be all that
suspicious, would they? But what the *burglar* forgot
was the old boy had been lying on his face long
enough for the blood to flow to the front of his
head.'

'Be a lot of blood lying about somewhere, though,
wouldn't there?'

'No, chief. Not a lot. Now I've seen plenty of head wounds. Traffic accidents, you know? Blood everywhere because the skull's *really* caved in. But this old bloke, well if he'd been thirty years younger he might not have died at all, see? Was there much blood on the beach?'

'Hardly any.'

The attendant permitted himself a smile of modest triumph. 'That's it then, chief. He didn't die there.'

'You ought to have been a copper,' said Roper solemnly.

'I tried,' said the attendant, wistfully. 'Too short.'

The official post-mortem examination was to take place here tomorrow afternoon. According to the chalked blackboard on the wall it was scheduled for half-past two.

'You've been a great help, son,' said Roper. 'Thanks.'

'My pleasure, chief.... Here, chief.'

Roper had reached the door, clasped the lever.

The attendant flashed his broken teeth in a huge grin. 'I can tell you who did it an' all, if you like.'

Roper smiled. The first time that day he had felt even the remotest stir of humour.

'The butler,' said the attendant, still beaming hugely. 'The butler did it. It's always the butler, eh, chief?'

ROPER STOPPED OFF to get himself a coffee from the machine in the corridor. It was still only three o'clock in the afternoon but already it was nearly dark and the street lights were coming on.

Miller was pinning up the scene-of-crime photographs on the cork board on Roper's office wall.

'How did you get on with O'Halloran?' asked Roper.

'Nothing we didn't already know,' said Miller, and Roper was quick to notice the hint of truculence in his voice. 'He left the house at five to eleven. On the dot, so he says. He also noticed that some kind of row had taken place between Winterton and Vestry. Didn't know what it was about, though.'

Roper hung up his sheepskin and carried his coffee across to stand beside Miller as he thumbed home the last tack in the last picture.

'How old is he?' asked Roper.

'About forty.'

'And what's he like?'

'Keen,' said Miller.

'A holy roller, is he?'

If Miller noticed the hardening edge in Roper's voice he gave no sign of it. 'No. Pretty normal.'

'Right,' said Roper. He took down a mouthful of coffee. 'So you *did* find out a few things that we didn't know already, didn't you, lad?'

Miller smouldered sullenly but said nothing.

'Did he kill George Winterton?'

'I didn't ask him.'

'Then you should have,' said Roper. Tomorrow, he would ask that very same question of Julian Winterton, and why it was that that gentleman had been excluded from his father's will. Roper had considered asking both questions on the way back in the car from the mortuary, but Winterton had still been floundering in the emotional backwash of his sudden and unexpected bereavement. Tomorrow, when he was a little more rational, Roper intended to interview him again.

With Miller still beside him, Roper sipped at his coffee and scanned the photographs. There were twenty or so of them, a grisly and colourful mosaic of glossy eight-by-tens, still slightly damp, still smelling faintly of acid from the darkroom.

From a full-face shot, Winterton stared out with one wide open eye and one that was closed to a slit that showed only a slender white crescent of the filmed eye beneath. About the dislodged false teeth the prissy little mouth was puckered with the radiating lines of old age. And Roper could not help noticing that it looked a cruel and vindictive little mouth, even in death.

The flashlit close-up that Roper had called for especially, of the back of Winterton's head, showed the fracture in sharper detail than had the diffused grey light of early morning on the beach. Through the thinning, blood-webbed hair, the almost circular flattening of the skull was clearly visible. Where the tightly-drawn skin had split at its centre the wound formed a rough approximation to a letter Y. As Dr. Harford had said, and the mortuary attendant had agreed in his eccentric, offbeat way, there was no penetration. Something heavy. Something flat. But what?

In the profile shots of Winterton's face, the flash had made more obvious the runnels of dried blood, the blood that had flowed forward from the back of his head to his temples. The capillary action of the hair had of course caused the blood to flow in several directions; but that forward flow to the temples predominated. Blood had no more dispensation than any other matter to defy the laws of gravity. Ergo:

it had not flowed upward while Winterton had lain on his back on the shingle at Monk's Cove.

It all seemed to Roper messy and unnecessarily complicated and in many ways downright inept. The trouble with murder was that it followed no regular pattern; unless you were dealing with a maniac. Murder was mostly a crime of the unique sort. Few people ever committed it more than once. And most murders were still what the police labelled as "Domestics". Husbands killed wives. Wives killed husbands. When, many years ago now, the very young Roper had come out of uniform and joined the C.I.D. the sage old inspector who had taken him under his wing used to propound a theory that there were only four likely motives for any kind of villainy: passion, panic, prejudice or greed. Find out which, and you were well on your way to nailing your villain.

'It's messy,' said Roper, aloud this time. 'And bloody clumsy.'

He took another sip of his coffee, then went and sat down at the desk. Miller joined him on the other side.

'Have you got a name, son?'

'Bernard,' said Miller, stressing the fullness of it. Not Bernie. Not even Miller's new young wife called him Bernie.

'Well, Bernie, what do you think?'

'I don't *think* anything. Not enough evidence.'

'People think all the time, son,' said Roper. 'You only stop thinking when you're bloody dead. You even think when you're bloody asleep.'

Miller stared sullenly back…. 'All right. If you're asking for my opinion—I *think* it's murder.'

'Premeditated?'

'Could be. But on the other hand, it might have been suicide.'

'Did you look at his shoes.'

'Yes.

'Then it wasn't suicide, was it?'

Two spots of colour blazoned high up on Miller's cheeks. 'It's still a *possibility*.'

'The hell it is,' said Roper. 'Think murder. How was it done? How could it have been done?'

'All right, then. *If*. Winterton was murdered at home, or in somebody else's. Whoever did it dumped the body down at the cove to make it look like an accident—or in the hope that the tide would come in and then take the body out and lose it.'

'Why d'you think he was murdered indoors?'

'The overcoat,' said Miller. 'And his scarf. No bloodstains. And none on the inside of the hat. That I could see.'

'So perhaps the hat was another bit of false bait.'

'Another?'

'His wristwatch,' said Roper. 'According to the mortuary attendant, Winterton had been on that beach a long time before half-past five. And there was plenty of life left in the spring. I checked.'

'Perhaps somebody wound it forward a couple of hours.'

'And then smashed it? It's too pat, son. A stopped wristwatch—stopped at the wrong time, I hasten to add; those keys in Winterton's pocket—the wrong pocket; Winterton changes his will just before Christmas, and last night, a few hours before he dies, he tells his solicitor he intends to change it again. The police doctor reckons Winterton died at one time, the mortuary attendant reckons some other time and the victim's wristwatch showed yet another time. And let's say, for argument, that Winterton *did* go out last night, let's say somebody called for him and drove him somewhere else in the small hours. Nobody heard him; at least his son and daughter-in-law didn't. And what man needs to creep out of his own house—unless, of course, he's up to no good. Which of course he might have been....'

But still it was all mostly supposition, and none of it with very much evidence to substantiate it. And Roper had learned a long time ago that it was never wise to suppose too far beyond the evidence at hand.

Miller produced his notebook and ran through the interview he had had with the Reverend Timothy O'Halloran while Roper had been along to the mortuary. There was nothing new. What O'Halloran had seen and heard at last night's dinner party was almost the same as Julian and Glenda Winterton had seen and heard. The only discrepancy was a small one of time. O'Halloran thought he had left Westwinds House a little *before* eleven o'clock last night, but Roper certainly was not going to make a liar of the man for the sake of a few minutes either one way or the other.

'Did he happen to notice any of that business between Winterton and Vestry, by any chance?'

'Yes,' said Miller, looking up from his notebook. 'Apparently he did. And he thought he might have heard the tail-end of a quarrel between Winterton and Coverley. —But he wasn't entirely sure, and he wasn't prepared to enlarge upon something that he might only have imagined.... I thought I'd take that up with Coverley when we see him.'

'What else?'

'Not a lot,' said Miller. 'Except an impression I got that the reverend gentleman wasn't too keen to talk about Mrs. Fowler. Nothing I could put my finger on exactly. If I had to put it into words, I'd have said that he was being politely evasive.'

O'Halloran thought that George Winterton was the salt of the earth.

'He almost ran out of superlatives,' said Miller. 'Winterton was on the church council at St. Philip's. He was also the treasurer of the roof-fund.' He flipped over a page of his notebook. 'And he was one of the governors across at the school— O'Halloran's the school chaplain, by the way…. Oh, yes, going back to the roof-fund, Winterton promised to chip in fifty of his own for every thousand pounds that was contributed by everybody else. So, like I say, O'Halloran thought the sun shone out of him.'

'Yes,' Roper drawled slowly, with a hint of irony. 'I can well imagine he did. And I suppose Mrs. Fowler lent an occasional hand with the flower arrangements.'

Miller shot an eyebrow.

Roper smiled without humour. 'So I'm clairvoyant, old son.' He reached out for the paper cup and slowly drained the last of the coffee from it.

Then he said, as he put the cup down again:

'How was O'Halloran evasive, exactly?'

'Well, for a start, when I asked him how long he'd known Mrs. Fowler he told me he couldn't quite remember—and didn't quite look me in the eye either. And yet when I asked him a few minutes afterwards how long Mrs. Fowler had worked for

Winterton, he told me six years. Straight off. No hesitation.'

'Did you press him?'

'There didn't seem any point. What he isn't is a killer.'

'But you don't *know* that, do you, son. For all we know he *could* be another Ripper on the run, right?'

Miller didn't answer.

'I'm not knocking gut-feeling, son,' said Roper, levering himself up from his chair and equally reluctantly steeling himself to go out into the cold again. 'Just so long as you don't mistake 'em for good solid evidence. Now let's go along and see our good friend the headmaster.'

SIX

VESTRY'S NEAT, grace-and-favour cottage stood a hundred yards or so down the lamplit lane from the school. At this time of day in the summer the lane would be awash with a home-going stream of clamouring boys, but on this wintry late afternoon all that reigned here was a desolate, snow-clad silence.

Miller pressed the bell. The front of the house was in darkness. Over to the left, almost lost among the shrubbery, a small brick building that had once been a stable had been converted into a garage. A thick drift of windswept snow lay piled against the bottom of its doors.

Miller gave another press to the bell. A faint glimmer of light shone through the stained-glass window beside the door, then a brighter one as whoever was coming to answer came along the hall. The door was opened against a burglar chain, and half a face regarded them cautiously through the vertical slit between the door and the frame.

Roper held out his warrant card. 'Detective Superintendent Roper, sir.... And this is Inspector Miller. He rang you earlier this afternoon.'

'Ah, yes, of course.' The voice was a little nervous, a little breathless. The slot of light narrowed for the few seconds it took Vestry to fumble the chain free. 'Do come in, both of you.'

The hall was narrow, and made narrower still by a jungle of bric-à-brac that gave it a flavour of the

nineteen-twenties and 'thirties; a bamboo-legged table, a huge and hideous green vase brimming with
plastic gladioli and dried pampas grass, and at either
side the walls were festooned with dozens of small
and precisely drawn watercolours of Redbury Sands
in all its seasons.

Clive Vestry too was small and precisely drawn.
Still dipping and bobbing nervously and with his
hands wrung together low down in front of him, he
said anxiously:

'I hope this visit isn't about any of my boys, Superintendent. They are all at home for the holidays,
you see. I couldn't possibly get in touch...'

His voice trailed away as Roper shook his head.

'No, sir,' said Roper. 'We're just making a few
enquiries; we think you might be able to help us.'

Several expressions fleeted one after the other
across Vestry's neat, pinched face. He was about
sixty, his greying hair tidily barbered. Oddly, he was
dressed for business, in a grey suit and waistcoat,
stiff-collared striped shirt and plain grey tie. It was
not the sort of garb a man would wear in his spare
time in his own house, and Roper presumed he had
decided to dress for this appointment as he probably
dressed for all his others.

'Yes...well...' began Vestry haltingly, still nervously rubbing his hands together. 'We'll go to my
study.... It's warmer.... Please,' he said, standing
aside and ushering them further along the cramped
hall to an open door whence a brighter light shone
out and lit the recess under the stairs, where there
was another hideous green vase filled with pampas
grass, and a scarlet-upholstered dining chair that
looked like a piece of Sheraton. And clean. Roper

noticed how scrupulously clean everything was. And his nostrils caught a waft of Turkish tobacco smoke that grew stronger as all three of them turned into the study.

Vestry's hands continued to rub and wring by turns as he bobbed into place behind his desk. A flap of his hand gestured towards the two chairs on its other side. A gas-fire glowed feebly in the hearth behind him.

'Sit—er—down, won't you. And take your coats off, if you wish.'

Both settled for only loosening them. The room wasn't all that warm, despite the gas-fire. The chairs were institution chairs, oak, straight-backed and slab-seated and highly polished, no doubt, by several generations of small boys squirming uncomfortably on them. Not, at the moment, that Vestry looked as if he could inspire terror into even the smallest of his pupils. He was, on the contrary, a man plainly disquieted and ill at ease. What he was not was a man physically capable of carrying George Winterton's dead body from the cliff road to the cliff edge; or if he had, then he certainly could not have done so alone. His desk-top was littered with sheets of white paper ruled into rectangles, some of which had been filled in with a neat block-lettered hand. They looked like classroom timetables. Vestry presently sat behind them like a timid mouse on a leaky paper raft that was in imminent danger of capsizing.

'Now—er—what can I do for you, Superintendent?'

Roper decided to get quickly to the nub of things rather than spend any time putting Vestry at ease. Vestry looked the type of man who thrived on nervous tension and was probably only really at ease with his staff and his pupils.

'We understand that you dined with Mr. George Winterton across at Westwinds House yesterday evening, Mr. Vestry. Is that right?'

Vestry's eyebrows came together. 'Why, yes,' he said. 'Indeed.'

'Mr. Winterton's dead, sir,' said Roper. 'We found his body on the beach at Monk's Cove early this morning.'

The skin went white and tight on Vestry's face; the hands gripping the arms of his chair tightened convulsively. 'Oh, my God,' he whispered. 'Are you sure?'

'We're sure, sir,' said Roper.

'Good God,' said Vestry softly. His hands released their grip on his chair and the colour began to return to his face. 'Forgive me,' he said. 'All this is something of a shock. I mean I was only dining with the man last night. He seemed perfectly well then.'

'Yes, sir,' said Roper. 'I'm sure he was.'

Vestry's reaction had been genuine; Roper was sure of that. Winterton's death had clearly been news to him.

Vestry passed the flat of his hand over his hair, then clasped his hands together on his blotter.

Yes, he agreed again. He had been a guest at Westwinds House last night, and his account of the evening was much the same as Julian and Glenda Winterton's and O'Halloran's. After dinner, talk had turned to local politics about which Vestry had little more than a passing interest.

'My life is here, Superintendent. Here and along

at the school.' He smiled apologetically. 'I regret to say that I have spent most of my life in scholastic institutions. It's a way of life all too easily acquired and very difficult to shrug off again. I am not a worldly man, and politics and those who practise them leave me utterly cold.'

'So you didn't enjoy the evening.'

'In all honesty, I did not. But then I rarely *do* enjoy what is called the social occasion.'

'Generally, sir,' suggested Roper, 'or last night in particular?'

'Oh, generally,' replied Vestry. 'But I was bound to go to Winterton's last night. He is—was, rather—on our board of governors. So I had to attend, you see. Courtesy, you understand. Even a schoolmaster has to keep an eye to business these days.'

'Had he been on your board of governors for long?'

'Oh, yes. Twenty years. A year longer than my own connection with the college. It was Mr. Winterton, in fact, who originally proposed me for the headmastership when Christopher Shipley retired. So, you see, my debt to him is—was—also a personal one.'

'Did you find him a likeable man, Mr. Vestry?' asked Roper.

Vestry spread his hands apart to the top corners of his blotter and drew it closer. It was obviously a gesture solely to buy time, and Roper guessed what the answer was going to be several seconds before Vestry's lips moved to frame it.

'No,' he said. 'At least—not a great deal.'

'Why, sir?'

Vestry stirred uncomfortably in his chair. 'There is an old saw, isn't there, about speaking ill of the dead. And I really cannot see how my personal opinion of poor Winterton could possibly help you, Superintendent.' His pinched narrow face lifted hopefully, as if he dearly wished this encroachment of the real world beyond his study window would recede and allow him to return to his timetables.

Roper smiled encouragingly, 'It all helps, Mr. Vestry,' he said. 'We're up against a brick wall, sir. We need to know the man; then perhaps we'll know better where to look for the right kind of motive. You see, sir, we can't be sure yet, but we suspect foul play.'

'Really?' said Vestry. 'Oh, dear. How very dreadful.'

But he was not surprised, Roper thought. Not the way he ought to have been. Death had surprised him. The manner of it scarcely moved him.

'I take it that this is strictly privy, Superintendent?' he asked at length.

'Subject to the fact that it doesn't turn out to be evidence, then, yes, Mr. Vestry.'

Vestry appeared to find something of absorbing interest about his thumbnails for a moment before glancing up again.

'Well...' he began hesitantly, 'he was not a kind man. He liked to use people. Find their weak spots, if you understand what I mean, and prey upon them.'

'You see,' Vestry began again, 'we are all vulnerable in some way, aren't we, Superintendent. You, the inspector here, myself. With respect, of course. We all have a blot of some kind on our escutcheons, don't we?' He looked hopefully at Miller, then at Roper, for reassurance, a thin smile on his mouth at this daring foray into humour. 'I, myself, am not a blameless man. I have not always done the right thing; all too frequently the wrong one, alas.'

Vestry's knuckles whitened as he clasped his hands tighter together. Whatever was on his mind was obviously difficult to phrase without the resolution of some very private and internal conflict. He was, Roper guessed now, close enough to sixty-five to be looking forward to retirement.

'Men who live alone are often objects of suspicion,' Vestry started again. 'Have you noticed that? A woman may live alone, and no ill is thought of her. But a man—now that's altogether a different kettle of fish, as they say. Bachelor schoolmasters and bachelor priests. People wonder, don't they?'

'I'm not entirely following you, Mr. Vestry.'

Another hiatus ensued. The elderly gas-fire behind Vestry popped twice in quick succession, then resumed its dolorous hiss. The room was plain, without either pictures or ornaments to disturb.

'Many years ago, Superintendent,' said Vestry at last, reluctantly coming to the point, 'I was involved in a scandal. A sexual scandal; or, to put it more accurately, a charge of homosexuality was levelled against me. I hasten to add that I was not guilty of the accusation.' The back of one thumb was nervously massaged by the front of the other. 'A boy, a senior prefect at my previous school, it was. I was younger then and homosexuality was not talked of quite as much in those days. I was, I may truly say, a dedicated teacher. And I was particularly sensitive to the agonies entailed by examinations—especially those which led to university entrances.

'The boy's name was Davidson, Superintendent. And he was everything that I had never been. A young Phoebus, good at games, and he played the cello beautifully. On the whole, a most *remarkable* boy. Gifted I would say. And I think I saw in him something that was not, in fact, there. The quality of humility.

'In short, I became his mentor. He was destined, subject to the fact that he went to one of the more established universities, for the Foreign Service. He needed languages—and that was the one area of his otherwise remarkable mind where there were grey spots.'

'So you coached him?'

Vestry sat back then, drawing his hands after him and letting them drop wearily into his lap.

'Exactly, Superintendent. My subjects were French, German and Latin. I coached him in all three. And, as well, I taught myself some Russian to further assist him. We became, in a way, companions. Oh, it's easily done, Superintendent, believe me,' he added wryly. 'One can get a heady feeling of triumph out of teaching, sometimes. A receptive young mind absorbing everything one pours into it. I suspect that it's all to do with vanity—in fact I'm sure it is.

'Well, the upshot was that I began taking him to London at weekends—Saturday evenings, usually—to watch films in the languages we were working on. And afterwards we invariably had supper somewhere before we caught the late train back to school. I enjoyed his company—oh, perhaps I was trying to recapture my own lost youth, however trite that might sound, but I really enjoyed being able to talk to someone without having the strictures of academe about me. To be able to talk without prudence—well, almost without prudence.

'I began to buy him textbooks—not to curry his favour, oh, no, but I needed to encourage him without appearing to be the heavy-handed schoolmaster. Can you understand that, Superintendent?'

'I do, sir.'

Vestry subsided deeper into his chair and his clasped hands reappeared to make a delicate prop for his chin.

'He stole money from me, Superintendent. Small sums at first. So insignificant, in fact, that I scarcely noticed them missing. Then larger sums; notes from my wallet. The sort of money that I could not help but notice had gone.'

'And you accused him?'

'Oh, no. Good God, no.' The wince that fleeted across Vestry's thin sharp face was close to pain. 'I avoided that at all costs. I thought it was a passing thing—it was so out of the character I thought I knew. Boys often do strange things, Superintendent, and often for reasons that they themselves do not understand. I took what I then believed to be the simplest course—I removed the temptation.'

'And at that point, I suppose, he actually asked you for money.'

Vestry's eyebrows rose in horrified surprise.

'You know?'

'Not specifically, sir,' admitted Roper. 'But it's been done before, and I've no doubt it'll go on happening. It's not an unusual story, believe me.'

Vestry appeared to draw strength from the reassurance. 'Money with menaces. I think that's what it's called. Blackmail. Davidson told me, quite plainly, that if I did not pay him what he asked for, then he would go to the headmaster with the story that our Saturday evenings in London were not entirely what they had seemed. I was astonished, Superintendent. I couldn't believe my ears. Nor could I even *begin* to believe that he would *actually* do what he threatened.'

'But he did?'

'Oh, yes. Indeed he did.... He was quite ruthless. And far less innocent than I who was more than twice his age. I had—still have, in fact, no real idea of what homosexuals actually *do*—if you follow me. I mean the down-to-earth mechanics of it.... But Davidson did. Oh, yes. Davidson *certainly* did.'

'Have evidence against you, Mr. Vestry, did he?'

'No, of course he didn't,' replied Vestry angrily. His clasped hands came apart, were bunched into fists, were crashed down on his blotter in outrage. 'Be damned if he had. But you see he didn't *need* it, Superintendent. It was only my word against his word, and in the closed little world of a public school the merest whiff of any kind of relationship between a master and a pupil is absolute death for the master.'

'Did it come to court, sir? Or were you dismissed—or what?'

'Oh, it's all very gentlemanly, Superintendent,' replied Vestry, now with a trace of gentle irony that was strangely at odds with the bitterness in his eyes. 'One is asked to resign—verbally, you understand. Nothing put into writing. So I resigned. I was helpless in the face of Davidson's vivid descriptions of what I had done with him. It was a year before I found even a temporary post—that sort of history follows one about. One needs references from one's former school.... Difficult to obtain you see, after all that had gone on. Of course, my former headmaster had to be careful—the law of libel and all that—and he did supply a reference, but of a kind. Guarded, hinting, everything between the lines if you take my point.

'Then one day, quite out of the blue, I received a letter from the board of governors of *this* school. It was an invitation to attend an interview for the post of a junior language tutor. The letter was signed on behalf of the board, and the then headmaster, by George Winterton—acting as deputy chairman. As I understood it, the chairman himself was away on business in the United States. Naturally, I was astonished. I couldn't believe my luck. For a whole year, I had moved from one temporary post to another—found for me by a teaching agency—and suddenly there I was with a promise of a whole new life staring me in the face. All I had to do was to attend an interview.

'As the post was only for a junior tutor, the vetting committee was composed of merely the headmaster, the deputy chairman of the board and the senior language tutor.'

'The deputy chairman still being Mr. Winterton?'

'Indeed,' replied Vestry. 'He was, I thought, a charming man—tremendously supportive. Not to labour the tale, through what I believed were Winterton's good offices, I was shortlisted, and eventually offered the post. Within two years I was an assistant housemaster. Another three and I was a housemaster, and four years after that I was the deputy headmaster. Dizzy heights, Superintendent, for a man who nine years before had been very nearly unemployable in the world of teaching.'

'Yes, I'm sure, sir,' Roper broke in patiently. 'And it's an interesting story. But, if you remember, my original question referred to Mr. Winterton. It's Mr. Winterton I want to know about. With respect, sir, we seem to be drifting from the point a little.'

'Winterton was the wretched boy's uncle, Superintendent,' said Vestry, on a sinking note of incredulity, as if, even after all these years, he still could not quite believe it. 'But I was headmaster when I finally found that out. At one of his dinner parties. He related an anecdote about a nephew of his who had been coerced—Winterton's word—into a homosexual relationship with a teacher at a certain public school. I could not help but recognise both the teacher and the school.'

Roper's interest flickered sharply to life again. 'Did he accuse you, Mr. Vestry? Directly?'

'He didn't need to, Superintendent. I lived in fear for months. Then one day, about a year after that particular party, he came here—to the house—and asked me to vote with him on a certain issue concerning the school finances. All the governors have two votes, you see, and the headmaster, who is an honorary governor, has one vote—and that one vote is often enough to sway things. I refused, told him that the project in question had my wholehearted disapproval. And that is when he came completely out into the open regarding the alleged affair between myself and Davidson.'

Remembering what Tasker had told him of the disposition of George Winterton's estate, Roper said:

'So Winterton must have had a brother or sister somewhere.'

'A sister,' said Vestry. 'She died. Ten—twelve years ago.'

'And what about his nephew?'

'I have no idea, Superintendent. For all I know, he might be dead too. And, God forgive me, I almost hope that he is.'

'So Winterton threatened you.'

'Yes. He told me that if I voted against the proposal I would be voting myself back on the streets—his exact words again, Superintendent. Back on the streets.'

'And you went along with him?'

'Superintendent,' said Vestry, 'I could do nothing else.'

'You didn't think of coming to us?'

'I didn't dare,' replied Vestry. 'As I tried to explain earlier to you, whether one is guilty or not, the seeds are sown, the talk spreads.'

'And was that the only time he made demands on you, sir, or did he try again.'

'Again,' said Vestry. 'And again and again. There was no end to it…. In fact, on several occasions I made myself very unpopular with the other governors because of it. I didn't dare go against him, you see.'

'So I presume that Mr. Winterton had some financial interest in the school, sir?'

'Oh, no,' replied Vestry. 'That is a condition of a governor's election. Absolutely no financial interest at all. But the school owns a lot of the land surrounding it and Winterton—by proxy, naturally—wanted to purchase several large portions, on three occasions. You know, don't you, Superintendent, that he was also chairman of the local council's planning committee....'

SEVEN

ROPER AND MILLER only had to prompt. Most interviewees had to have every last detail prised from them; others had to have their answers elicited with all the subtlety and delicacy of a locksmith picking an unfamiliar mechanism with only a paper-clip. Vestry fell into neither category. Vestry wanted to talk, and Roper was prepared to listen because what were coming from Vestry were answers to which Roper realised that he did not know even half the questions.

Vestry, for some time, had stood looking out of the study window at his darkened garden. Between two of his fingers was clamped a loosely-packed Turkish cigarette which he drew on from time to time while its aroma, sickly sweet and pungent, slowly filled the room. He had at last reached the subject of the brisk exchange between himself and Winterton that Julian Winterton had partly overheard last night on his way to the kitchen.

'He was going—as he put it—to reveal me, Superintendent.... He told me that I was a bloody old queer who'd had a damned good run for his money. They were his exact words.' All Roper could see of Vestry's face was his profile and his reflection in the dark panes of the window, but the headmaster's repugnance at having to repeat Winterton's words was plain.

'To what end was Winterton making this threat, Mr. Vestry?'

Vestry sighed, and finally turned away from the window and his reflection and came back slowly to his chair. He sat down tiredly. One of his hands floated forward and its edge swept across his blotter as if he had sleepily noticed a speck of dust on it.

'There was a ring-road proposed to the north of the town, Superintendent. But I expect you know that.'

The ring-road was common knowledge. It had been promised to Redbury Sands for the last twenty years and was at last coming to fruition. A public enquiry was due to be held only a month or so hence to discuss the three possible routes it could take. And, according to Vestry, common to all three alternatives was a roundabout at Laurel Spinney at the northern edge of the school grounds.

'It will be, I understand, quite a large roundabout, absorbing some three or four acres of the spinney.' Vestry broke off for a moment to fumble about under his timetables for an ashtray. 'Laurel Spinney belongs to the school,' he went on, absently tapping ash from his cigarette. 'It was willed to us by a certain Mrs. Blakemore. Both her sons were killed in the last war, and both were educated here at the school. She willed it to us as a memorial to them, and we installed a small tablet there as a token of our own. The boys use it a great deal. They practise their orienteering there. Our Army cadet force·uses it for manoeuvres. Our Boy Scout troop for field and woodcraft skills. And at least twice a week in spring and summer a master takes one or the other junior classes there for nature and biology tutorials. So, you see, we put it to the sort of use that I imagine the good Mrs. Blakemore had in mind for it. As a piece of land, it was not worth a tremendous amount; but to the school its value is inestimable.'

But with the roundabout in the offing, Laurel Spinney was no longer a piece of semi-waste land. Its value had taken a leap on the grand scale.

'And Winterton wanted to buy it—through a nominee, of course—*before* the enquiry took place. That was particularly important. And naturally, he wanted it for a price that even I knew was ridiculous, so that when the roundabout is finally agreed upon, and made the subject of a Compulsory Purchase Order, which it undoubtedly would be, Winterton could sell the land to the Department of Transport and thereby make for himself a profit that I can only describe as outrageous.'

But by this time, by now careless of the consequences, Clive Vestry had begun to resist George Winterton's threats. And last night, in Winterton's study, he had finally dug his heels in. Vestry ground out his cigarette as if it were a substitute for his dead oppressor.

'I told him that if he were looking for a casting vote in favour of his agent buying that particular parcel of land, then he would have to look elsewhere. I told him that I had reached the end of my tether. There was nothing more he could do to frighten me. That he could tell his spurious stories about me to whomever he wished. But that if he did, and I found out that he had, I would take an action for slander against him.

'He laughed, Superintendent. Told me that I had reached, as he put it, the end of the line. Then he tapped the glass of his wristwatch and told me that I had just twelve hours to come up with the goods. If I did not, he told me, before the end of the Easter term I would be out of the school on my neck. My something-neck—I will not debase myself by repeating the particular adjective he used, Superintendent.'

Roper could well imagine. And he was sufficiently aware that he was not so entirely without sin himself as to have no sympathy for the abused and oppressed little man who sat across the desk from him. In his darker moments, Vestry might have indulged in fantasies of murder. He might even now *be* the murderer; but even if he was, and only half of what he had told them about Winterton was true, then Roper still could only think of Vestry as victim rather than villain.

'You say he gave you twelve hours, sir,' said Roper. 'Does that mean you had an appointment with him this morning?'

'Yes,' said Vestry. 'At half-past ten. And I telephoned the house at that time to reiterate my intention of ignoring his threat.... But his daughter-in-law answered and told me that he wasn't there.'

'Did he call you H.M. ever, sir?' asked Roper, as the possible connection with Vestry and the entry in Winterton's desk diary occurred to him.

'Yes. He did. H.M. For headmaster. Frequently. Especially at governor's meetings. Our colleague, the H.M. To mock me, you see; although none of the other governors ever knew that. His humour could be most cruel and acidulous sometimes.' Vestry subsided back into his chair. 'And you know, Superintendent, when his daughter-in-law told me that he was not at home, I was angry at first. There was so much I wanted to say to him. But after I had put down my telephone, I began to hope that he was on his way here—to see me. I *would* have killed him, I think. How, I don't know. But here, alone with him, I really think that I was in a mood to kill him.'

At this point, Vestry's gaze lifted and fixed itself on Roper's. It remained like that, penetrating and four-square for several long seconds; until Roper narrowed his eyes and said quietly:

'And *did* you kill him, Mr. Vestry?'

Vestry was not put out. He slowly shook his head, with what was almost a hint of wistfulness. 'In my mind, Superintendent, a dozen times over the last few years. But physically, no. If I had, believe me, I would have told you so.'

And he would have, thought Roper.

'I'm surprised you stayed at the house last night; after the quarrel.'

'I wasn't going to,' said Vestry. 'But then young Winterton brought me over a very large whisky, and Mr. and Mrs. Tasker joined me. And I decided that to stay would be effectively to show Winterton my colours. To spite him, as it were.'

'And you left the house when?'

'Soon after half-past twelve—although I didn't finally get away until nearly a quarter to one. My car wouldn't start. Mr. Faulkner, of the *Argus,* very kindly had a look under the bonnet for me and diagnosed a faulty starter motor. Eventually, he and Julian Winterton and Mr. Coverley gave me a push to get me going. That was very kind of them, I thought.'

'So you got back here to the cottage when?'

'About one o'clock. A few minutes either side perhaps.'

'And you didn't go out again?'

'I had no cause, Superintendent. It was cold, and frankly the evening had exhausted me.' Then he added, with another of his wistful smiles:

'And I live here alone. So I have absolutely no alibi.'

THEY WERE LEAVING, standing in the cramped hall at the foot of the stairs, buttoning their coats and pulling on their gloves.

'Nice set of pictures you've got here, Mr. Vestry. Local artist, is he?'

'My own work,' said Vestry. 'Although I admit to no more than a modest talent. A hobby, that's all.'

'Very nice indeed, sir,' said Roper, although, closer to, the pictures were too tightly drawn and too meticulously detailed for the medium in which Vestry had chosen to paint them. They were, however, another small insight into his character. Whenever Clive Vestry had entered the world he was, and always would be, a Victorian.

Vestry had no objections to having his car examined.

'Whenever you wish, Superintendent,' he said, as he held open the front door for them, 'I certainly can't drive it anywhere at the moment. And as I've already told you, I've absolutely nothing to hide.'

The door closed behind them, and the dark and the cold encompassed them again. With the dark, the settled snow had developed a frozen crust that crackled underfoot like fragments of glass.

'Do you reckon he has?' asked Miller, when they were safely out of earshot along the path.

But Roper was still in no mood to commit himself about Vestry either one way or the other. Vestry's look of shock at hearing of Winterton's death had looked convincing; and so had his subsequent relief, the almost euphoric rebound that had so loosened his tongue. On the other hand Vestry had a classic motive. Although, if he had killed Winterton, he could never have managed to get the body to Monk's Cove on his own. He would have needed an accomplice. And Vestry had struck Roper as a lonely man, probably by choice, and a man who would have shared his murder with no one. Amidst such cerebral seesawings, Roper chose to leave the options open for a while longer.

As they stepped out into the lane the constable who had driven them here was just climbing out of the car.

'Just had a buzz over the radio, sir,' he called, over the car roof as Roper and Miller approached him across the grass. 'Forensic's come up with something useful on that stick.'

MORE THAN USEFUL. Something to gloat over. The first real piece of honest to goodness evidence that had turned up all day.

Roper passed one Polaroid photograph across to Miller, then another; but he retained the last one on his own side of the desk and peered at it more closely through a magnifying glass, although the photograph, taken through a microscope, was well magnified already.

Its centre of focus was a protuberant knot in George Winterton's walking stick. It was surrounded by a circle of minute splinters, although at this magnification the whole looked like a miniature volcano, the top of which was crowned by a *cheval de frise* of sharpened stakes.

And there, snagged among the sharpened stakes, was the honest to goodness piece of evidence. A tuft of cream-coloured fibres. The fibres themselves were now secured in a polythene envelope stapled to the back of the photograph. To the naked eye the tuft was scarcely visible, an inconsequential fragment, barely even palpable except by the most delicate rub of a thumbnail over the plastic film that protected it.

At length, Roper handed the photograph across to Miller then sat back in his chair and digested the forensic laboratory's report on the inconsequential wisp.

It was, the report stated categorically, a fragment of a cotton and nylon mixture, tough and hardwearing. The inner fibres were clean, the outer ones soiled, which meant that the tuft had become snagged on the stick, but very recently, possibly in the last twenty-four hours. A sample had been submitted to tests on a spectrophotometer. Predominant among the traces of various substances adhering to the outer layer of fibres were the salts commonly exuded in human perspiration—and automotive engine oil.

Less categorically, but equally trenchantly, the report then went on to suggest that such a nylon and cotton mixture was of the type and texture—and weight—and colour, frequently used in the manufacture of driving gloves, the sort with leather palms and a knitted, open-work back, a theory further reinforced by the presence of the engine oil.

According to the report, most of the fingerprints on the handle of the stick had been smudged beyond reasonable identification, except one. And that one was a thumbprint. A woman's. But Roper set little store by that. Mrs. Fowler had bought the stick for Winterton as a Christmas present. Ergo: it needed only the slightest imagination to guess that this sole latent print was hers. If it was, that particular piece of evidence put the investigation no further forward.

If he viewed it pessimistically, the same could be said of the tuft of nylon and cotton. If it had been snagged from a driving glove, and that glove had belonged to either Winterton or Mrs. Fowler, then he and Miller were up another dead end.

But instinct made him cautiously optimistic. Winterton's neatly barbered hair and immaculately manicured fingernails both indicated a fastidious man. Those bony well-kept fingers had never seen the inside of a grubby driving glove, and men with Winterton's kind of money rarely serviced their own motor cars. And women, with a few exceptions, even more rarely.

He unwound himself from his chair and went back yet again to the photographs on the wall.

There was a snag; there always was. Practically every car driver in the country owned, or had once owned, a pair of leather-palmed and knitted-back driving gloves.

The telephone jangled on the desk behind him. He heard Miller pick it up and answer it.

Mrs. Fowler was back from Bournemouth.

EIGHT

FOR THE SECOND TIME that working day, Miller hauled on the handbrake outside Westwinds House. Interestingly, he had followed two fairly recent sets of tyre-tracks ploughed muddily into the snow all the way from the gateway. One set went off to the right, towards the hidden garage, while the other pair terminated beneath the rear wheels of a scarlet Volvo estate car parked carelessly askew in front of the porch, as if its driver had been in a hurry to get here.

The front of the house was prodigally lit. As they approached the porch, as if to disabuse at least some of this prodigality, the shadow of a man moved across the window of the room to the right of the front door, with an upraised arm to close the curtains. He stilled briefly as he caught sight of Roper and Miller and said something over his shoulder to whoever was in the room behind him. Miller thought he recognised him: Coverley, from the pottery.

It was Mrs. Fowler herself who let them in. Roper had expected a hard-faced chatelaine in black bombazine and with a ring of keys hanging from her belt, or something very like that. But Mrs. Fowler was nothing like that. She was somewhere in her late forties, robustly attractive and still a long way yet from going to seed. She was still wearing her tweed outer coat and a woollen scarf, even though it was a good ten minutes since she had telephoned

the station to say that she was back from Bournemouth.

Her glance at their identity cards was only an ab-
stracted one.

'Yes,' she said. 'I'm sure you're who you say you
are.... Mr. Coverley's been telling me what's happened. Please come in, won't you.'

She showed them into the sitting room where they
had interviewed Julian Winterton and his wife that
morning. Coverley was standing four-square across
the fireplace with his back to it, burly and bearded
and wearing stained jeans under an expensive-
looking navy-blue driving coat. He was obviously
here as Mrs. Fowler's protector.

She introduced Coverley, but a couple of barely
audible grunts were all that came from Coverley.

'Please sit down, won't you,' said Mrs. Fowler,
and took her place in the armchair nearest the window. Coverley moved sideways and joined her on
the arm of it. He eyed them inimically as Miller took
out his notebook and gave a pump to his pencil.

'I'm proposing to stay,' he said. 'I take it you
have no objection.'

'If I do, I'll let you know, Mr. Coverley,' said
Roper, and effectively dismissed him out of hand by
switching his attention less frostily to Mrs. Fowler.

'I've no doubt all this has come as a shock to
you, Mrs. Fowler. I'm sorry to have to question you
at all, but I'm sure you understand why.'

'Yes.... Of course,' said Mrs. Fowler, gazing
down at her clasped hands. 'Glenda...Mrs. Winterton, told me the news when I came back. Mr. Coverley has just been filling in some of the details. I

understand you think that Mr. Winterton was murdered.'

Coverley had lit a small cigar. He shook out the match and tossed it into the fire where it flared brightly again before it was consumed.

'When did you last see Mr. Winterton, Mrs. Fowler?'

'This morning...early...or perhaps I should say last night.... About five-past or ten-past two. Something like that.'

She had brought Winterton's cup of hot chocolate into the lounge—this room—at about two o'clock, returned to the kitchen to put away the last of the crockery that had been used for last night's party, then come back in here to put a few glasses back in the sideboard. Then she raked the fire down; Winterton apparently had a phobia about fire. They had talked, for perhaps two or three minutes, exchanged good nights, then she had gone upstairs to bed.

'Did you hear Mr. Winterton come up?'

'Yes,' she said. 'A few minutes afterwards. But then, when I was in bed, I thought I heard him go downstairs again.'

'And what time would that have been?'

She wasn't sure, but thought that something like a quarter of an hour might have gone by since she had heard him come up.

'So about half-past two,' suggested Roper. 'Something of that sort.'

'Yes,' she agreed. 'Probably.'

She described the earlier events of last night much as everyone else so far had. Quiet. Food, drink, gossip; no feathers had been ruffled, nobody had raised his voice. It was all, so far as Mrs. Fowler had been aware, an amicable gathering.

At five to twelve, she and Winterton had charged all the guests' glasses and at midnight they had all toasted in the New Year.

'So you didn't know that Mr. Winterton had had a quarrel earlier in the evening with one of the guests?'

She looked surprised. 'No,' she said. 'No, I didn't.'

'He had two,' broke in Coverley. 'Or would you still rather I stayed quiet.'

'Yes, I would rather, Mr. Coverley,' said Roper, with a touch of flint in his voice. 'I'll get round to you afterwards. Mr. Winterton was fairly sober, was he, Mrs. Fowler; when you last saw him?'

'Yes. He'd drunk very little all evening. According to his doctor he wasn't supposed to drink alcohol at all. He suffered slightly from angina.'

'Did he take anything for it?'

'Yes. Occasionally. Some kind of spray that he had to squirt under his tongue. But, as I said, it wasn't all that serious.'

'Do you know if he suffered an attack last night?'

'No,' she said. 'I'm sure he didn't.... Unless it was after he went to bed. Although when the attacks came they were usually in the morning, soon after he'd got up. Rarely at any other time.'

Roper steered her back to last night. She ran through the order of the guests' departures with little difficulty. O'Halloran had left around about eleven; he had had a service to conduct. Next to leave had been Mr. Vestry, the headmaster; that had been at about a quarter to one. She particularly remembered

Vestry's leaving because of the trouble he had had starting his car. The Taskers left next, then Jack— Mr. Coverley here—then the Faulkners. It was by then about ten-past one.

Mrs. Fowler and Glenda Winterton had then gone out to the kitchen and taken the china and glasses out of the electric dishwasher, made sure everything was dry and stacked them all on the kitchen table. Mrs. Winterton had then brewed some coffee in the percolator. She took one cup into the lounge for her husband, drank her own in the kitchen, then poured another for herself which she took upstairs to bed with her.

'About what time was that?'

Mrs. Fowler shrugged. 'I can't be sure, exactly. But about half-past one, I suppose.'

'Then what?'

'Oh, I pottered about the kitchen, tidied up so that I didn't have to face a mess in the morning. That sort of thing, you know?'

'And where was Mr. Julian Winterton during this time you were working in the kitchen?'

'In here. Talking to Mr. Winterton. So far as I can remember, he went up to bed a few minutes before I took Mr. Winterton in his chocolate. I heard him say good night.'

'You say they were talking, Mrs. Fowler.'

'Yes.'

'How?'

She frowned, looking up at Coverley, but sensibly he stayed silent.

'I'm not sure what you mean.'

'Were they talking quietly or heatedly?'

'Quietly. Yes. Definitely quietly. Something to do with young Mr. Winterton's business, I think.'

They had been sitting on opposite sides of the fireplace, Winterton with a cigar, his son with a cigarette and the cup of coffee his wife had made for him.

'So Julian Winterton went upstairs at about what time?'

'Oh, about ten to two, something like that.'

'And you went to bed at about ten-past?'

'Yes.'

She was definitely a handsome woman, blonde, good bones, healthy skin. Not cut-glass by a long chalk; in her voice were traces of the north London suburbs, where Roper himself had first seen the light of day, but she had plainly taken a great deal of trouble to erase most of them. It was fairly obvious why Coverley should be attracted to her.

Like his jeans, Coverley's shoes were spattered with white crusty patches of what looked like china-clay. His shirt-collar and pullover were frayed and the fact that he was wearing his working clothes under his driving coat probably meant that he had driven here post-haste from his pottery in response to whatever summons Mrs. Fowler had sent him.

'You say you heard Mr. Winterton go back downstairs at about two-thirty. Did you hear him come back up again?'

'No, I didn't.'

Coverley sent a cylinder of ash from his cigar winging into the fire. 'Perhaps he didn't go back upstairs,' he proposed. 'I mean, he was found on the beach in his dinner togs, wasn't he? I should think that meant that he never went to bed, wouldn't it?'

'You seem to know a great deal about all this, Mr. Coverley.... How come?'

Coverley's hostility surfaced again. He took a lengthy pull on his cigar and let the smoke curl slowly out again. 'I had a drink with Hugo Faulkner at lunchtime. You gave one of his reporters the story.'

Roper stayed eye to eye with him a moment longer, then dropped his gaze back to Mrs. Fowler.

'I understand you bought Mr. Winterton a walking stick for Christmas, Mrs. Fowler.'

'Yes,' she said. 'One of those rustic knobbly ones with a hooked handle.' She drew a semi-circle in the air. 'Like that.'

'It was a hawthorn,' said Coverley. 'I was with Mrs. Fowler when she bought it.'

'So you could both identify it?'

Each thought they could.

'He put it in the rack in his study,' said Mrs. Fowler. 'I saw it there yesterday afternoon.'

'Would you mind going into the study now, Mrs. Fowler; to see if it's still there.'

'Yes, of course.' She rose and went out into the hall. When her footsteps had receded, Roper said:

'What was *your* relationship with Mr. Winterton exactly, Mr. Coverley?'

'Business,' replied Coverley.

'Can you expand on that?'

Coverley didn't reply at once. Then he shrugged.

'The pottery's had a bad time during the recession. I needed money to expand. I knew if I could get into the European market I could keep my head above water. Then when I did manage to get in, I found that I couldn't turn the goods out fast enough, and that caused a cash-flow problem. I needed an automated kiln and the bank wouldn't lend me the money because I was already too deeply in hock with them. It was a bloody vicious circle.'

'And you asked Mr. Winterton for a loan?'

'Hell, no,' retorted Coverley, with a sneer of disgust. 'I wouldn't have asked Winterton for anything. But Grace did—Mrs. Fowler. And one afternoon Winterton turned up at the works with a cheque for twenty-five thousand pounds.'

'Which you didn't turn down, I take it?'

'Oh, I wanted to, believe me. And I damned nearly did.' Coverley tossed the end of his cigar into the fire. 'But I'm a realist. And that morning, I'd got an order for sixty thousand pounds worth of stuff from West Germany—and I also had twenty people, most of whom have worked for me for years, whose livelihoods are sunk in that pottery as much as mine is.'

'But with that order as collateral you could have gone back to the bank, surely?' said Roper.

'Yes, and I wish now that I had,' replied Coverley. 'But with the bank there was paperwork. Could have taken a week or more. And there was the entire cost of that oven sitting there in Winterton's hand. As it stood, I could go upstairs there and then, and pick up the telephone and order the bloody kiln. I tell you, it was like Eve and the bloody apple.'

The loan had not been repaid exactly.

'It wasn't that sort of loan,' said Coverley. 'Winterton wanted to buy into the firm. A seven and a half per cent share in the profits. At that time it would have been seven and a half per cent of not very much.'

'But it isn't now?'

'Hell, no,' said Coverley. 'The pottery's been on the up and up ever since.'

'And Winterton was drawing a regular dividend?'

'Damned bloody right, he was.'

'Couldn't you have bought him out?'

Coverley stared darkly back. 'Don't think I didn't try,' he said. 'I was practically prepared to go broke again to buy the old bastard off. But he wouldn't have it.'

'And yet you were invited here to dinner last night, and you accepted the invitation. Seems odd, that, Mr. Coverley.'

Coverley jerked his head fractionally towards the door to the hall.

'I needed to see Winterton about Mrs. Fowler and me,' he said. 'It seemed as good a time as any. We both wanted to get it over with, you see. Grace and me; we had to be sure which way the old bastard was going to jump.'

For a second or two Roper was caught off kilter. There was another complication in the air. He could almost smell it, almost as strongly as the lingering fragrance of Coverley's cigar.

'Jump, Mr. Coverley? How do you mean exactly?'

'Blackmail,' said Coverley. 'He was blackmailing Mrs. Fowler.'

NINE

COVERLEY'S NEW and unexpected revelation generated a long silence after it, so that Mrs. Fowler's return from the study was given a touch of theatre.

'Was the stick there, Mrs. Fowler?'

'No,' she said, with a lift of her shoulder. 'Apparently not.'

Roper waited until she had resumed her chair and Coverley had lit a cigarette for her.

'You were saying, Mr. Coverley,' he said. 'Something about blackmail.'

'It's down to Mrs. Fowler here,' said Coverley. 'Perhaps she ought to tell you.'

AND MRS. FOWLER DID tell them. It took some time, and a lot of encouragement from Coverley, and what emerged was an even more unsavoury picture of George Winterton than Roper already had.

He said:

'But you were acquitted, Mrs. Fowler, and it was a long time ago.'

'She still wanted to keep it quiet, damn it,' interrupted Coverley. 'And that isn't easy in a tin-pot town like this.'

'But you could have moved on, Mrs. Fowler. Why didn't you?'

'Because I was settled here, because I'd got to know Mr. Coverley by this time.'

'And I couldn't exactly sell the pottery and pack

my tents, either,' Coverley broke in again. His driving coat was over the back of the chair now, and Roper saw how tightly his shirt was strained over his chest and shoulders. A big, powerful man. Built like a professional wrestler, quick to anger, a man who could easily have hefted George Winterton's negligible weight clean above his head and hurled him a dozen feet outward into the fresh air of Monk's Cove.

'So the old bastard had both of us in a cleft stick. The more we wriggled the tighter we were trapped in it.... And old George enjoyed every damned minute of it. Frankly, I'm glad the old swine's gone. And I don't give a damn if you write that down and quote it in court.'

'Glad enough for you to have killed him yourself, Mr. Coverley?'

Coverley stretched a thin smile. 'I've often thought about it lately. But no, I didn't.'

Roper returned the smile. 'I'm pleased to hear that, sir.... Tell me, Mrs. Fowler, I'm still not with you on this blackmail business; what was Mr. Winterton after, precisely?'

'I can answer that,' said Coverley. 'He wanted her in his pocket, like he wanted everyone else. He was plainly and simply a sadist, a latter-day bloody Hitler.'

'So not money?' said Roper. 'And not sex?'

It was Coverley who bridled at that, and Mrs. Fowler who replied equably: 'It was neither. As Jack said, Mr. Winterton was a sadist. He enjoyed power over people, however small that power was. For him that was satisfaction enough. He collected other people's sins like other men collect stamps. Ask the other guests who were here last night; I'm sure most of them will tell you the same.'

Well, not quite all, thought Roper, but three out of five so far was a pretty fair proportion. Although he had to own to a private doubt or two about Mrs. Fowler. She simply did not look like a victim of tyranny. She had taken off her coat while she had been looking for the walking stick; the smart, grey barathea suit she wore beneath it looked as if it had been tailored for her. Ergo: she either had money of her own, or Winterton paid her uncommonly well.

'So he simply wanted you to stay here and look after him.'

'Yes,' she said. 'That's all.'

Roper remembered what Haggerty had told him: said she was his housekeeper and general factotum; 'but I got the impression that she was a hell of a sight more than that...' Well, perhaps Haggerty was wrong; but, at the earthiest level, Mrs. Fowler exuded a strong sexual attraction and was definitely not the sort of woman that any red-blooded male, even an elderly one, could live alone with for very long without making some kind of overture to.

'Getting back to this morning, Mrs. Fowler. Before you went out, did you have any idea then that Mr. Winterton wasn't in the house?'

'I thought he might not have been.'

'Why did you think that?'

'His keys. They weren't in the hall.'

Winterton, apparently, had an obsession about not going out without his keys. So he kept them on the half-moon table beside the telephone. He picked them up from there on his way out, and dropped them back there on his way in.

'Always?'

'Invariably. It had become a habit.'

She sounded very sure.

She had left for Bournemouth that morning at eight-fifteen, which was just about the time that Roper and Miller had arrived at Monk's Cove. She had driven herself there in Winterton's car, which she had his carte blanche permission to use more or less whenever she needed. Winterton himself had stopped driving some years ago. Mrs. Fowler wasn't sure, but she thought that he had not had a driving licence for several years now because of his angina.

'But you didn't think it was unusual that Mr. Winterton should have been up and out that early? Especially after the late night he'd had last night?'

'No,' she said. 'Not at all. He always had two or three hours sleep in the afternoon; and he was always up in the morning soon after seven, regardless of what time he went to bed.'

'But he was out of the house, Mrs. Fowler,' Roper insisted. 'Didn't you think that was odd? Considering how cold it was early this morning?'

'Well, yes,' she answered eventually. 'I suppose I did.... But I wasn't his keeper exactly. He was my employer and this was his house. He came and went as he pleased.'

'So you weren't concerned?'

'No,' she replied. 'Why should I have been?'

'If we can hark back a bit; you told us you heard Mr. Winterton go back downstairs round about two-thirty this morning.... And you say that you didn't hear him come back again. Are you absolutely sure about that?'

'Positively.'

'When you heard him go down…supposing he'd left the house then? Would you have known? Heard the front door closing behind him, perhaps? Anything of that sort?'

No, she had not. Nor, necessarily, would she have. Her flat was at the upstairs rear of the house. And, anyway, Winterton's going downstairs was the last sound she recalled hearing before she fell asleep.

'And you didn't hear a car at all? Someone who might have called for Mr. Winterton to take him somewhere?'

'I heard nothing. I've told you. Really.'

MRS. FOWLER brought in a wooden tray with tea things on it for herself and Coverley, and laid it down at one end of the coffee table.

'Can you remember what time you left here this morning, Mr. Coverley?' asked Roper.

Coverley finished lighting another cigar. 'Five-past…ten-past one,' he said. 'I didn't exactly look at my watch.'

'You left just before Mr. Faulkner, that right?'

'No,' countered Coverley. 'After.'

'But Mr. Tasker's told us that you called good night to him from your car, while Mr. Faulkner was still on the front porch talking to Mr. Winterton.'

'Yes, that's true,' agreed Coverley. 'But then I noticed that I'd left one of my driving gloves behind. It must have fallen out of my pocket.'

'So you went back for it?'

'Yes.' Coverley reached out for the cup of tea that Mrs. Fowler had just poured for him. 'I found it on the floor under the table in the hall where Winterton kept the telephone.'

'What sort of gloves are they, sir?' asked Miller.

'I told you,' replied Coverley impatiently. 'Driving gloves. Leather palms, knitted backs. The usual sort.'

'May we see them, sir?'

Grudgingly, and by dint of some juggling with his cup, saucer and cigar, Coverley reached along the back of the chair to the pocket of his driving coat. He fumbled out a pair of gloves that he tossed across ungraciously to Miller's lap.

Miller separated them and passed one across to Roper. It was exactly the right sort of glove, with a light-tan leather palm and a cream-coloured knitted back. The palm was a little grubby, but it was scarcely creased, and the stitches of the knitted back all seemed to be intact. It had obviously seen little use.

'When did you buy these, Mr. Coverley?'

'I didn't,' said Coverley. 'They were a Christmas present from Mrs. Fowler.'

'Did you have a similar pair before that?'

'Yes.' Coverley had had an exactly identical pair. When Miller asked him what he had done with them, Coverley replied that he had tossed them into the toolbox in his Volvo to slip on when a dirty job like a roadside wheel-change came up.

'I suppose you'd like to see those, too.'

'Later, Mr. Coverley,' said Roper. 'On our way out. We may even take them with us, if that's all right.'

Coverley shrugged dispassionately and took a sip of his tea.

'Tell us, Mr. Coverley, what time did you get home this morning, after you'd left here?'

Coverley shifted to one side as Mrs. Fowler sat down again in the chair beside him with a precariously balanced cup and saucer. 'I didn't go home,' he said. 'I went straight down to the works.'

'At one o'clock in the morning?'

'Of course at one o'clock in the morning,' retorted Coverley. Like his repertoire of facial expressions, the range of his voice varied only between irritability and blistering contempt.

The manufacture of pottery these days, he declaimed testily, was a continuous process, a production-line job, which could not be allowed to come to a stop for a mere bank holiday. Especially now that the automated kiln had been installed. It was a voracious machine, fed with slipware at one end and spewing out the fired product at the other to be decorated and glazed.

'Turn the oven off, and you have to hang about for a couple of days waiting for it to heat up again. And that's a bloody waste of bloody expensive gas. So I keep it stoked up. And because I can't afford to pay double-time, I do the holiday work myself.... I keep a campbed rigged up in my office.'

'Anyone see you in the pottery? Guard? Night-watchman?'

Coverley used neither. They were too expensive and non-productive. It had been cheaper to have a security alarm installed. It was hooked up on a direct line to the police station switchboard.

'So nobody saw you there.'

'If you're asking if I've got an alibi, the answer's no.'

According to Coverley, having arrived at the pottery in the early hours, he did not set foot outside it again until half-past twelve this very afternoon, when he had crossed the street to the Mariners' Arms for a bite of lunch. It was in the lounge bar of the Mariners' that he had met Hugo Faulkner who had told him of Winterton's death, and the grim possibility that Winterton may have been murdered. He and Faulkner had had a few jars together, and Coverley had then returned to the pottery at about one forty-five. He had checked the automated kiln, then gone upstairs to his office until Mrs. Fowler had rung to tell him that she was back from Bournemouth and that the police were on their way to interview her.

He further insisted that between three o'clock and seven o'clock that morning he had been asleep on his camp bed in his office.

'You mentioned earlier that you'd had a quarrel with Mr. Winterton last night. Something to do with yourself and Mrs. Fowler.'

'Yes. Stupid, really,' said Coverley, retreating a little. 'I'd arrived early to have a few words with him about Grace and me, and he pretended that he didn't know what I was talking about. I lost my temper.'

The exchange had taken place in the hall, mostly in undertones because Julian and Glenda Winterton were frequently in the offing.

'I asked him for five minutes in his study. Just the two of us. He asked me why, and I told him that I knew he had some kind of hold over Grace here, and that I knew what it was. And that he was about to lose it because Grace and I intended to get married at Easter.'

'And how did he react to that?'

'Viciously,' replied Coverley. 'He was a sarcastic little tyke, or perhaps you haven't found that out yet. He said: "How very quaint. I didn't think you were the marrying kind." I asked him again to step into the study with me. He told me that he hadn't the time, and, anyway, we had nothing to talk about that couldn't wait until the morning. Then he turned his back on me. That's when I lost my temper.'

'And?'

Coverley hunched his burly shoulders. 'I grabbed him. His arm. I didn't hurt him. I told him we had plenty to talk about and top of the agenda was blackmail. I'll give him credit, he kept his cool. He just looked up at me and told me not to be bloody ridiculous. So far as I was concerned, that did it.'

'Did what?' asked Roper.

'I blew my top,' said Coverley. 'I started to bundle him towards the study. Only we didn't get there.... I suddenly realised that Julian was answering the door to O'Halloran. I was still clutching a handful of Winterton's sleeve. I think O'Halloran saw us.'

'What happened then, Mr. Coverley?'

'Nothing,' said Coverley. 'That was the end of it. It was a waste of time anyway.'

'And yet you stayed here, Mr. Coverley. You sat at Mr. Winterton's table, ate his food and drank his tipple. I'm surprised you did that.'

'I couldn't do much else,' retorted Coverley. 'Not without skulking out with my tail between my legs, and I certainly didn't intend to do that.'

'So you stayed out of spite, as it were?'

'Yes,' Coverley admitted grudgingly. 'I suppose you could say that.'

'You weren't exactly a friend of Mr. Winterton's, were you, sir,' said Miller. 'I mean you've already told us that.... And from what I read in the local papers you and he had a good few slanging matches across the council chamber.' Winterton had been a High Tory; Coverley billed himself as an Independent Socialist; a polarity of political opinion that had several times recently thrown council meetings into what the *Argus,* with its usual over-emphasis on the scarcely more than mundane, described as 'total disorder.'

'Yes,' agreed Coverley. 'Damn right we did. The man was a bloody Fascist.'

'Had he ever invited you here before?'

Coverley gave a brisk shake of his head. 'No,' he said.

'Then why do you think he invited you here last night?' asked Roper.

There was a momentary lull. Then Mrs. Fowler said:

'That was my doing, Superintendent. Mr. Winterton asked me to send out the invitations. I included Mr. Coverley. I pretended afterwards that it was a mistake, that I hadn't noticed the cross by his name in Mr. Winterton's address book.'

'Which means I was strictly persona-non-bloody-grata,' Coverley muttered in the background.

Roper ignored him.

'Why did you do that, Mrs. Fowler? I mean Mr. Winterton was bound to find out, wasn't he?'

'I was trying to engineer some kind of truce between Mr. Winterton and Mr. Coverley,' she said. 'I thought that once Mr. Coverley had received an invitation, Mr. Winterton could hardly withdraw it. And that once Jack—Mr. Coverley—was here, in the house, he would be able to talk to Mr. Winterton.'

Winterton had found out about the illicit invitation when Coverley's acceptance came through the post.

'And what did he say?'

'Oh…he was angry at first, then he was amused.'

'She means cynically amused,' explained Coverley, sotto voce; and again Roper ignored him.

'Are you saying, Mrs. Fowler, that Mr. Winterton left it to you to determine who came here to dinner last night?'

'No,' she said. 'Not quite.'

Apparently guests came to Westwinds on a rota system; according to the order in which they appeared in Winterton's address book. Fortuitously, for Mrs. Fowler at least, Coverley's name occurred in the book between Tasker's and O'Halloran's. The address book was not the usual sort, with an alphabetical index down the side, merely a small red pocket book that Winterton carried about with him and scribbled names and addresses in from time to time. Mrs. Fowler fetched it from the study and Roper thumbed interestedly through its dog-eared pages. It went back years by the looks of it and many of the names in the first few pages had been struck through, their owners presumably deceased. Its price pencilled on the fly-page, ninepence, was further testimony to its antiquity. None of the handwriting in it was Mrs. Fowler's.

And there was a ballpoint pen cross beside Coverley's name.

Roper handed it back to her.

'We were talking earlier about Mr. Winterton's keys,' he said. 'You told us that he used to keep them on the table in the hall whenever he was in the house. Tell me, can you remember if you saw them there late last night?'

She frowned for a moment, then said: 'No, when I went around locking up I don't think they were. I can't be sure, mind, but I'm fairly certain that they weren't.'

'How about you, Mr. Coverley?'

Coverley shook his head. 'Sorry,' he said. 'I didn't look.'

WINTERTON'S BEDROOM was at the back of the house, a large airy room with a huge bay window that looked out over the grounds, white lawns, an ornamental pond and the long shadows of the trees cast by the lights from the house. In the distance, a necklace of red tail-lights crawled sluggishly up the downs towards Dorchester before disappearing slowly over the crest.

The room was sparsely furnished. A set of oak-faced wardrobes was built into the wall opposite the window and a military style dressing chest stood beside it. On top of it, an electric shaver in its box and a pair of silver-backed hairbrushes stood in front of the tilting mirror. The bed, a single divan, was neatly made up with one corner of the covers turned back.

'Did you make the bed this morning, Mrs. Fowler?'

'No, I didn't.' Winterton insisted on his bed being aired when he had risen from it. He threw back the bedclothes when he got out of it and they had to stay that way until the late afternoon when Mrs. Fowler was then allowed to make it tidy again. It was a regular part of the household routine, a lot of which seemed to be based on Winterton's sundry quirks and foibles.

'So it wasn't slept in last night?'

'I'm positive,' she said. 'Mr. Winterton certainly wouldn't have made it himself…. He was scarcely house-trained. It was as much as he could do to put his own clothes in the wardrobe.'

Roper heard the note of rancour but passed no comment. The top drawer of the dressing chest was locked. The one beneath contained only under-clothes.

There was a door to the right of the head of the bed. It led out on to a landing. A flight of narrow, carpeted stairs to the right went down, Roper guessed, to somewhere near the kitchen. To the left, a passage with a door at its end led back towards the front of the house, presumably opening out on to the landing of the main stairs. There was another door opposite.

'Is that your flat, Mrs. Fowler?'

'Yes.'

'May I see it?'

She skirted him and held the door open and switched on the light.

This was her sitting room. It was stylishly but comfortably furnished, with a view of the grounds and the downs similar to the one from Winterton's bedroom. Two armchairs were drawn up close together facing the television set in the corner. A low, glass-fronted bookcase took up most of one wall, its top decorated with a menagerie of china and glass animals, and a few Christmas cards. The general impression Roper received was one of homeliness; the kind of ambience that a lonely man would find welcoming on a cold winter's night. Through the still open door he could see straight into Winterton's bedroom. It looked, he thought, a most convenient arrangement.

At the far side of the room another door opened into a bedroom. It was chintzy-pretty, with most of its floor taken up by a double-divan and a long white wardrobe. The bric-à-brac on top of the dressing table by the window was arranged with an almost military precision, tall flasks and jars at the back, short ones at the front, two hairbrushes side by side and not so much as a paper thickness out of parallel, the kind of orderliness with which a soldier might lay out his equipment for a kit-inspection—or a prisoner his cell for governor's rounds.

'Were these rooms always here, Mrs. Fowler, or are they part of a conversion?' asked Roper, meeting her glance through the mirror of the dressing table.

'They were converted,' she said. 'This room and the sitting room used to be one large bedroom. Mr. Winterton had it done soon after I started here.'

'And how about the stairs?'

'Yes,' she said. 'Those, too.'

'Expensive, I should think.'

'Yes,' she said. 'I believe it was.'

He picked up one of the hairbrushes and turned it over. It was scrupulously clean, without a single strand of hair caught up anywhere. Its companion was the same, and yet neither was particularly new.

'Do you do all the housework yourself, Mrs. Fowler?'

'No,' she said. 'A woman comes in three mornings a week to do all the major cleaning. I look after all the small things.'

'And see to the cooking?'

'That wasn't difficult. Mr. Winterton ate very simply.'

'Except for the occasional dinner party, like the one you had here last night.'

'Yes,' she said. 'But they were only once a month affairs. Nothing very difficult.'

He met her eyes in the mirror again as he put down the hairbrush. 'Were you his mistress, Mrs. Fowler?'

'No.'

'Ever?'

'No,' she said. 'Not ever.'

He turned to face her, trying to read something in her expression that might have given the lie to her quiet denial; but there was nothing to read. It was almost as if she were merely an interested watcher on the sidelines rather than a possible participant; and perhaps she was. But what she certainly was was the nearest thing to an intimate confidante that Winterton had.

TEN

THEY WERE BACK in the narrow passage at the head of the stairs to the kitchen.

'You say you heard Mr. Winterton go back downstairs at about half-past two. What did you hear exactly?'

'I heard his bedroom door close, then a few seconds afterwards I heard the stairs creak. I also heard the light switch click. This one.' She touched the light switch on the wall beside her.

'You heard that through two closed doors?'

'No,' she said. 'One. I always leave the door between my sitting room and my bedroom open.'

'And you're sure he went down to the kitchen?'

'I'm positive,' she said. 'If he'd gone down to the front of the house I wouldn't have heard the stairs creak.'

'Let's try that, shall we.'

Roper returned to her bedroom, leaving open the door between that and her sitting room, and called for her to go through the motions that she thought Winterton might have made in the early hours of this morning.

He heard the click of a door latch—just heard, so that he wondered if he would have heard it if he hadn't been listening for it. The snap of the switch was scarcely more audible. But the creak of a stair that followed shortly afterwards was quite unmistakable. It was followed almost immediately by another, although the second one was not so loud; but both were distinct. So, if Mrs. Fowler were to be believed, at some time around half-past two George Winterton had gone downstairs for some reason, perhaps to the kitchen, perhaps to his study. For what reason probably only George Winterton would ever know.

Mrs. Fowler was waiting for him at the foot of the stairs, where a new doorway had been knocked out to give access into the kitchen, which was fitted out like an advertisement in one of the Sunday supplements, with cupboards and work surfaces all along the walls, and a cabinet-style refrigerator and a massive electric cooker both of which would have serviced a small industrial canteen.

The door to the garden opened on to a short stretch of patio. At the end of it, a couple of flagged steps led down to a similarly flagged path that was the way through the trees to the garage.

'Was this door locked when you came down this morning?'

'Yes,' she said. 'And bolted.'

'So if Mr. Winterton *had* gone out last night it would have to have been through the front door—or one of the french windows along the back here. Right?'

'It would have to have been the front door,' she said. 'Apart from this door, all the doors at the back of the house are kept permanently locked. I have the only keys.'

'I noticed some bolts on the front door... Were they on or off when you went out?'

'Off,' she said. 'They were another reason that I guessed Mr. Winterton was out.'

Her gaze was quite steady, quite frank. It was easy to see how she might have fooled that jury at the Old Bailey, if indeed she had fooled them. She looked strong, too, physically. She looked as if she might tip the scales at somewhere between eleven and twelve stones. She could not, without some help, have tipped George Winterton over the cliffs, but she was certainly robust enough to have killed him with little effort. And possibly in this house. Somewhere. And her likeliest accomplice was Jack Coverley.

'Do you wear driving gloves, Mrs. Fowler?'

'Yes.'

'May I see them, please.'

They were in the pocket of her tweed coat now hanging on the newel-post at the bottom of the stairs. They were entirely the wrong sort of glove, made of leather throughout and with vented backs. She had never, so she said, owned a pair with knitted backs and leather palms. Roper handed them back to her.

Coverley and Miller were still in the lounge. Coverley, crouching in front of the hearth, was banking up the fire with more logs.

'May we look at those old gloves of yours now, Mr. Coverley?'

'Sure,' said Coverley, levering himself up slowly with his hands cupped on his knees. 'But they won't help you.'

Roper and Miller waited while Coverley got into his driving coat, then followed him out to the scarlet Volvo parked in front of the porch. Its rear hatch, Roper saw now, was held shut with a twist of wire looped around the rear bumper. Coverley untwisted the wire and raised the hatch and bent inside to haul forward a plastic tool-tray.

There were no gloves. There were spanners and screwdrivers and an aerosol of de-icer and some bits and pieces of metal castings that might have been parts of a carburettor. But there were no gloves, even when Coverley, finally exasperated, upended the box and shot the entire contents out into the boot.

'Not there, Mr. Coverley?' asked Roper.

'You can bloody well see they aren't, can't you?'

'But they were. So you said.'

'They were,' insisted Coverley. 'I chucked them in there on Boxing Day. I remember doing it.'

'So why aren't they there now?'

'If I knew that, I'd have already told you, wouldn't I?'

'When did you see them last, Mr. Coverley.'

'When I chucked them into the toolbox,' said Coverley. 'Boxing Day.'

'And you haven't been to the toolbox since?'

'No,' said Coverley. 'I've had no reason.'

Roper felt the cold seeping up through the soles of his shoes, through his clothes, and with it the first real grounds for suspicion that had confronted him all day. Coverley had had a pair of knitted-backed driving gloves. He no longer possessed them, or if he did he wasn't going to admit it. Such a pair of gloves had been used to handle Winterton's walking stick. Ergo...

'I want those gloves, Mr. Coverley.'

'Look, I've just told you. I've lost the damned things.'

'And I'm not arguing with you, Mr. Coverley. I'm

simply asking you to find them. And when you have I'd like to see them.'

SOME TIME HAD PASSED. Both Roper and Miller had taken off their outer coats and looked settled in for the night. Coverley and Mrs. Fowler had separated and were sitting in the two armchairs facing each other.

'A good employer was he, Mrs. Fowler?'

'Yes. Or so I thought. Until he found out that I was seeing Mr. Coverley. Then he changed.'

'How?'

'Oh—small things at first,' she said. 'Sulking. Like a little boy. He did a lot of that.... I didn't realise what the cause was at the time.'

'So you hadn't kept your relationship with Mr. Coverley secret?'

'No,' she said. 'Certainly not. Why should I? But on the other hand I certainly didn't tell Mr. Winterton that Jack and I were going about together, either. It was none of his business.'

'When did you find out that he knew?'

'Last spring.'

One evening in late April, Coverley and Mrs. Fowler had been to a cinema in Bournemouth, and afterwards had dinner at a hotel on the seafront. On the outskirts of Redbury, on the way back, they had stopped at the traffic lights at the eastern end of the esplanade, neither of them aware that Winterton, in a taxi, had pulled to a stop behind them. When Mrs. Fowler arrived back at Westwinds, Winterton had beaten her by a short head and was waiting for her here in the lounge, still in his overcoat.

'You had a quarrel?'

'No,' she said. 'It wasn't like that. Not at first anyway. He told me that he'd seen Jack and I together coming back into town. He told me that Jack was a thoroughly bad lot where women were concerned and that I'd do well to keep him at arm's length. I told him that what I did outside was my own affair.'

It was at that juncture that Winterton's attitude abruptly changed.

'He told me that he knew who I was, and that if he cared to put it about I'd find life extraordinarily difficult; those were his exact words. He said that he'd gone to a lot of expense and trouble to fit me in here and he didn't intend to have me running off and making a fool of myself with Jack Coverley.'

'And you accepted that?' asked Roper, on a rising note of disbelief.

'I had to,' replied Mrs. Fowler. 'Or at least I pretended to. It was much the easier way. I had a good job here, virtually the run of the house, and to be fair to Mr. Winterton he paid me the kind of salary that I could never earn anywhere else as a housekeeper. I loathed him after that—and I might as well admit it—but I decided to make the best of it, at least for the time being. I thought a year. By that time Mr. Coverley's firm would be well on its feet again, and we intended to get married round about then.'

'So you were acting a part here, Mrs. Fowler, that right?'

'Yes,' she conceded. 'I was. But it did no one any harm, least of all Mr. Winterton, and it gave Mr. Coverley and me a chance to get ourselves sorted out.'

'And enabled you to approach Mr. Winterton about that loan to Mr. Coverley.'

'There was nothing dishonest about that,' she said. 'Mr. Winterton was quite prepared to make the loan and Mr. Coverley had every intention of paying it back.'

And Roper agreed with that. It wasn't dishonest, not strictly speaking. Just immoral and devious and downright sly.

Then he took them through it all again, with an occasional question from Miller to quicken the momentum and confuse them a little. But neither shifted from their original stories, even when Roper tried to disorientate them more with a back-track or two and a zigzag or two. At one point, straight from the shoulder, he asked Grace Fowler if she and Coverley were lovers.

'And I mean in the modern idiom, not the Victorian one.'

'Don't answer that, Grace,' snapped Coverley. 'It isn't relevant, and I'm bloody sure he's no right to ask it.'

'I didn't put the question forward as a matter for discussion, Mr. Coverley. I asked it because it's relevant—*and* pertinent to our enquiries. For all I know you might be the protagonists in a crime passionel. I mean, you might be, mightn't you? And if you won't tell me, that leaves me to guess. Right?'

'Yes, we are,' said Mrs. Fowler tiredly. She had produced a handkerchief from somewhere and was absently rubbing the palms of her hands with it. 'And we have been for some time. I expect you'd find out sooner or later anyway.'

'Thank you, Mrs. Fowler. That's all I wanted to know.' Then, to Coverley, Roper said:

'*Was* it a crime passionel, Mr. Coverley?'

Coverley's entire face and throat tightened in anger, so that for a second or so Roper thought that Coverley was going to launch himself at him and do him a mischief. Then he subsided again and his face slackened.

'No,' said Coverley. 'It bloody well wasn't.'

'Thank you, Mr. Coverley,' he said. 'I'm obliged to you.'

When Roper eased himself up from the settee Coverley looked faintly surprised. 'Is that it?' he said, as if he had just bought something and suddenly discovered that he had been short-changed.

'Yes, that's it, Mr. Coverley,' said Roper, reaching to the back of the settee for his sheepskin coat. 'For the time being anyway.... But we'll probably be back after the post-mortem. That's tomorrow afternoon.' He smiled without humour as he ran finger and thumb up his coat to button it. 'So don't leave town, as they say, will you? Either of you?'

'I don't think you have the authority to tell us that, either,' said Coverley rising slowly out of his armchair.

Roper stretched his smile a little wider as he tucked his muffler deep into his coat collar. 'Joke, Mr. Coverley,' he said, and suddenly let the smile cloud over again. 'But not entirely. I'd like to come and talk to you both again tomorrow evening. Loose ends. That sort of thing. You know?'

ELEVEN

'TELL US ABOUT last night, sir. What you heard, what you saw.'

Faulkner spread his hands. 'Out of the ordinary? Absolutely nothing.'

Faulkner and his wife had arrived at Westwinds soon after Coverley—eight o'clock, or thereabouts. For the rest of the evening, his account was more or less a repeat of Vestry's and the Wintertons'.

The Faulkners lived almost as lavishly as Winterton had, and certainly more pretentiously, and there was a newness about their possessions that gave the impression that they were striving desperately to keep up with whatever the current trend happened to be, stacked hi-fi, flat-screen television, video-recorder, a gas-fire with dummy logs that flamed and glowed like the real thing. All of which were anachronisms in the lounge that was on two levels and decked out to look like a whitewashed Tudor barn, complete with fake oak beams and too many fake horsebrasses.

Faulkner himself was somewhere in his late forties, incipiently florid and with that sweaty over-fleshiness that sometimes catches up with rugby players when they finally give up the game and prop up the club-room bar instead. His wife sat in the armchair opposite him, a small, faded woman with dark moist eyes and her hands clasped nervously on her lap.

'So you didn't notice anything unusual? Nothing at all?'

'No, not really,' said Faulkner. Then he withdrew a little, and raised a hand and with a thumb and forefinger gave an outward stroke to each wing of his moustache. A moustache that was darker than his hair so that it did not look quite real but rather a theatrical contrivance. 'Except that I think—but only think, mind—that Winterton and Vestry might have had a row.'

'You heard it, sir?'

'No,' said Faulkner. 'I didn't hear anything. But after dinner it was pretty obvious that the two of them weren't talking to each other.'

'And you didn't notice anything else?'

Faulkner shook his head.

'This quarrel, sir, did Mr. Vestry mention it to you when you gave him a hand with his car?'

'No. He wouldn't. He's not that sort.'

'What time did you and your wife leave West-winds House last night, sir? D'you remember?'

'I forget,' said Faulkner. 'About five-past one. Something of that sort.'

'It was ten-past, Hugo,' said Mrs. Faulkner timorously. And there was an immediate and very nearly a shocked silence because, until now, she had made no contribution to the proceedings at all.

'Ten-past, Hugo,' she dared to say again. 'I looked at my watch. I remember.'

Faulkner gazed across at her with mild surprise. Then smiled testily at her. 'So it was *ten*-past one,' he agreed. 'Or so my good lady assures us.'

'And you got home when, sir?' asked Miller.

'About twenty-past.' Faulkner shot a glance at his

wife, as if he were daring her to contradict him again. But she didn't.

'Did you go out again, Mr. Faulkner?' asked Roper.

'Good God, no. Too cold. We came in. I had a nightcap. The wife went straight up to bed. I stayed up for about half an hour, then followed her up.'

'Is that right, Mrs. Faulkner?' asked Roper, more with a view to irritating Faulkner than seeking verification from his wife. It wasn't dispassionate as it ought to have been, nor was it just, but Roper's judgement of Faulkner had been too immediate to ignore. He was too hearty, too bluff, one of life's boisterous back-slappers.

'Yes, I think so,' replied Mrs. Faulkner. She glanced tentatively across at her husband. 'Should you mention that 'phone call, Hugo? It might be important.'

He sighed. 'Oh, hardly,' he said, with a kind of weary fortitude. 'For pity's sake, Dolly, these gentlemen are probably tied up in enough knots as it is. Don't let's waste any more of their time, eh, old darling.'

'No, sir,' insisted Roper, with a winsome smile at Mrs. Faulkner. 'We'd like to know. What 'phone call, Mrs. Faulkner?'

'It was kids,' broke in Faulkner. 'Kids at a party.'

'I asked your wife, sir. What time was this, Mrs. Faulkner?'

But, disappointingly, she did not know. She had been deeply asleep, had surfaced briefly at the distant ring, had heard the rumble of her husband's voice answering someone, then dropped off again almost immediately.

'The time, Mr. Faulkner? Do you remember?'

'Oh, God knows,' said Faulkner. 'I didn't look. I was half asleep myself. I traipsed downstairs, picked up the receiver. It was some kids; I could hear pop-music in the background—glasses, voices. This girl, boozed to the gills by the sound of her, asked to speak to somebody called Daphne. I told her there was no Daphne here, she'd got the wrong number; and she laughed and asked me why the hell I'd bothered to answer the 'phone if I was the wrong number. I was bloody annoyed, I tell you.'

'Yes, sir, I'm sure you were. But let's get it straight if we can. You went to bed at ten to two, say. Were you asleep when the 'phone rang?'

'I really can't see that it matters,' protested Faulkner. 'I told you, it was a hoax. Kids.'

But yes, he agreed. Pushed to a guess, the hoax call must have been five minutes either side of ten to two.

'When you left Mr. Winterton's house last night, sir,' said Miller. 'Did you notice anything on the table in the hall? The one near the front door.'

Faulkner stroked his moustache again and pursed his lips. 'Well...the telephone, of course, but that's always there.... A glass ashtray.... Oh, yes, and a bunch of keys.... And there was a glove *under* the table.... A driving glove, I think.'

'Might the keys have been car keys, sir? Did you notice?'

'No,' said Faulkner. 'Definitely not. Door keys. One was a Chubb.'

'And you were the penultimate guests to leave. That right?'

'No,' said Faulkner. 'We were the last, weren't we, Dolly?'

'No, Hugo.'

Another of those awful silences as Faulkner fixed his wife with a glass-hard stare across the hearthrug.

'No, Hugo,' repeated Mrs. Faulkner. 'The superintendent's quite right.... Jack Coverley left after us.... I am right, Hugo,' she persisted, in the manner of a woman who had been told all too often that she was not. 'I remember distinctly; as we were driving away Jack got out of his car and went back to speak to George at the front door. And you said—and I remember that distinctly too—you said: I wonder if Coverley's going back to give old George a punch on the nose. You *did* say that, darling. Really.'

Faulkner stirred sheepishly in his chair. 'Yes,' he said. 'I'm sorry. I'd forgotten about that. I remember now. Coverley *had* started his car, but then we saw him get out again and he went back to see Winterton about something or other.'

'Did you see him go into the house?'

Neither had.

'No,' said Faulkner. 'Sorry. The last time I saw him, he was still at the door.'

'The remark you passed to your wife about Coverley taking a swing at Mr. Winterton, sir. Were you serious, or was it a joke?'

'Joke,' said Faulkner. 'Of course it was a joke. It's just that Coverley's always got a face like bloody thunder. And he and Winterton didn't get on.'

'Really, sir,' Roper chipped in quickly. 'You know that for sure, do you?'

'Gossip's my business,' said Faulkner. 'I'm tuned in to it all the time. It's what sells newspapers.'

'Yes, sir,' said Roper drily. 'But gossip's one thing and facts are another.'

But Faulkner, when it came to the point, had no facts, only the exchanges of Coverley and Winterton across the council chamber that were reported in the columns of his own newspaper.

ROPER SAID:

'Do you happen to own a pair of driving gloves, Mr. Faulkner? Or any other kind of glove made of cream-coloured cotton?'

Faulkner shook his head. 'No. Sorry. I wear rally gloves. Leather. Vented backs.'

Yes, thought Roper. You would.

'No, dear,' Dolly Faulkner had leaned forward anxiously again, 'you do have ones like the superintendent says.' And before Faulkner could contradict her, she hurried on, 'the ones Linda bought you for Christmas. Linda's our daughter,' she explained, shrinking back into her chair again.

Two spots of colour blossomed high up on Faulkner's cheeks. 'Right again, aren't you, old darling. But I haven't worn them and I haven't seen them since Christmas Day.'

'I put them away,' said Mrs. Faulkner. 'They're in the drawer with your cardigans. In the wardrobe.'

'Can we see them. Please.'

'Sure,' said Faulkner. 'No problem. Well, go on old darling. Chop-chop.' He clapped his hands together to hustle her along, a gesture so preposterously arrogant that Roper thought that it was some kind of private joke between them; that it was not so funny as Faulkner thought was made evident by his wife's long hard look of distaste before at last she did rise from her chair and go out to the hall and up the stairs.

Faulkner seemed blithely unaware of his crassness. He sat with his head tilted to one side as he listened for his wife's footfalls to diminish up the stairs and along the landing. Then his eyes hooked on to Roper's as he hunched forward in his chair and smiled lopsidedly.

'The thing is,' he began, dropping his gaze and lifting it again, so that Roper, rightly as it turned out, prepared himself for another shiftily imparted confidence. 'The thing is—you'd have found out eventually, so I might as well tell you myself. Truth is though, I'd rather the wife didn't know. At least, not yet.'

His eyebrows rose questioningly, seeking the implied reassurance. But none was forthcoming. Somewhere upstairs a door slid on metal runners and perhaps realising that he did not have a lot of time before his wife came back, he went on quickly, 'I borrowed twelve K off old George last night...'

'K, sir?'

'Thousand,' explained Faulkner. 'All fair and above board, of course. I gave him a proper IOU. Nothing dodgy, that's what I'm trying to say.'

He smiled hopefully, but again met no response. So far as Roper was concerned, when a man borrowed a substantial sum of money from another who was subsequently—or perhaps even consequently—murdered, such a set of circumstances was extremely dodgy indeed.

'For what, sir?'

'I owe my newsprint suppliers. It's not that the *Argus* isn't selling, but I've just sunk most of my spare cash into starting a freebie. A weekly advertising tabloid. Drop it free into all the local letterboxes once a week. All the revenue comes from selling ad space. It'll be a sure winner, no doubt about it. The only snag is that it needed a lot of cash to set it up. I've got this place...' Faulkner took the house in with a comprehensive swivel of his eyes '...mortgaged up to the chimney-stacks. That's the bit the wife doesn't know about.... At least, not yet.'

He sat upright and drew back quickly into his armchair as his wife's tread sounded along the landing and down the stairs.

The gloves were still in their sealed polythene envelope, uncreased, never worn.

MILLER AND ROPER rose as Mrs. Faulkner came back into the lounge. She had put on a quilted outer coat and a headscarf and was tugging on her gloves.

'You're sure there's nothing else you want to ask me?'

'No, madam. Thank you,' said Roper. 'Have a good evening.'

She smiled with a disconcerting brightness, so that Roper wondered briefly if her proposed jaunt to the cinema with a woman friend was all that it seemed.

'Yes. Thank you. I shall.' The smile faded. 'We'll probably go on to a meal somewhere, Hugo. So don't wait up, will you?' And before Faulkner could think of a reply she had turned on a heel and was gone and the front door had closed behind her with a thud. Silence again.

'I understand that Mr. Winterton once levelled an accusation against you, Mr. Faulkner. That you'd set fire to your printing works yourself.'

Faulkner smiled. 'Yes, I know he did. But it was a joke. And he was well boozed at the time. But that's the sort of man he was. A stirrer. He didn't mean anything by it.... He was harmless—once you understood him, that is.'

'And you understood him? You got on well with him?'

'Well, no. Not exactly. No one did.... But certainly well enough.'

'Well enough for him to have lent you money. After the fire.'

'Yes,' agreed Faulkner. 'I borrowed money off him. But so what? It was a business arrangement. Good for Winterton, good for me.'

'You could have gone to the bank.'

'Hardly,' retorted Faulkner. 'Not with the insurance company dragging their heels the way they were. Banks—insurance companies—they're all in cahoots with each other. And I was running out of time. I had an edition to get out in five days—or go broke. I found a printer who was prepared to run it off for me. But when he heard the insurance people were sending down a second team of investigators he backed off. Thought I wouldn't be able to pay him, you see. I don't blame him. I'd have got cold feet myself in the circumstances.'

And as it had been with Coverley, so it had been with Faulkner. At the exactly opportune moment, George Winterton had arrived on Faulkner's doorstep with a cheque in his hand. A loan, a loan that in a few months, when the insurance company had still been shaking its corporate head in doubt, Faulkner had been only too eager to exchange for a sleeping partnership on behalf of Winterton.

'I've been looking at the files on that fire, Mr. Faulkner,' said Roper. 'As I understand it, there was a drum of highly inflammable ink-thinners close to the electrical junction-box where the fire started.'

Faulkner sank back tiredly into his armchair. 'Now look, Superintendent. I've told your people, the Fire Brigade, and God knows how many deputations from the insurance company: those drums were always kept in that corner. Usually, there were half a dozen of them; on the night of the fire there was only one. Now if I'd really wanted to burn the works down I'd have stacked the place high with the damned thinners. Wouldn't I?'

'I don't know, sir,' said Roper. 'You tell me.'

'I am telling you,' said Faulkner. 'And anyway, when the fire started I was across at Winterton's place and had been all evening. Ask my wife, ask Mrs. Fowler.'

ON THE TELEPHONE beside the front door were a pair of leather rally gloves weighted down with a set of car keys.

'Yours, sir? Can I take a look at them?'

The gloves were flashy, white leather with red facings over the backs of the fingers. The tag on the key ring carried a Rover emblem.

'Were you wearing these gloves last night, Mr. Faulkner,' asked Roper.

'No, I wasn't,' said Faulkner. 'I couldn't find the damned things. I'd stuffed them into my raincoat and hung it up in the wardrobe. I found them there this morning.'

'So you weren't wearing gloves at all last night?'

'No,' said Faulkner. 'We were running late. I didn't have time to look for them. And look…' he moved closer and dropped his voice a fraction, '…don't get me wrong, that money I owed George…I wasn't trying to welsh on him…he'd agreed to wait for it until the middle of the year…. And I wasn't the only one, you know. I know for a fact that Jack Coverley owed the old man more than a few shillings. But, that said, it wouldn't have been worthwhile either of us knocking him off, would it? We both had copper-bottomed agreements, signed and sealed. I mean we both still owe Winterton's estate, don't we? No way out of that, is there, I mean to say?'

'No, sir, indeed there isn't,' replied Roper. His voice sounded pleasant enough, but if at that moment he had been doodling a list of suspects then Faulkner's name would have been bracketed with Jack Coverley's—at the head of the list.

Like his oak beams and his horsebrasses, he was a fake. Not necessarily a villain but definitely a fake. Roper had spent too much of his life raking over the human race's midden-heaps and opening their cans of dirty worms not to recognise one when he saw one. Faulkner was the loud-voiced teller of dirty jokes in saloon bars, the perennial, if balding, sixth-former.

TWELVE

ROPER FETCHED himself a coffee from the machine along the corridor and drank it standing by his office window. It was coming up for eleven-thirty at night. The snow had stopped and the air was as clear as crystal. There was hardly any traffic about and few pedestrians and it was almost as if the entire town had shut up for the night and gone home to bed. The traffic lights went through their sequences like actors rehearsing in an empty theatre, and in the shopping precinct across the plaza a mosaic of lights shone in shop and office windows with an equal lack of purpose.

There was one more person to be interviewed, the young woman that Mrs. Fowler had hired from the agency to wait at the table last night, but Roper held out little hope of learning anything new from that direction. She could be shelved until tomorrow. Miller, after typing out a précis of the notes he had made during the day, had gone home for the night and Roper would soon do the same. The back of his eyes prickled and his brain felt as if it could easily slip out of gear.

According to how he looked at it, the exercise with the dogs had come up with nothing at all—or a very great deal. Their handlers had let them roam to and fro across the cliff top for the best part of an hour; if George Winterton's scent had been left there, then the dogs' delicately twitching noses had failed to find it. And since they hadn't sniffed it out, it probably wasn't there; and if it was not, then Winterton had definitely not gone down that path under his own steam. Ergo…

It would have been easy at this juncture to jump to a few conclusions. Coverley, Faulkner, Vestry, Mrs. Fowler—and Julian Winterton too, perhaps—all had had some kind of motive for putting George Winterton out of the way.

Both Coverley and Faulkner could have managed it alone, and so could Julian Winterton. Mrs. Fowler would have needed an accomplice, and it was a possible rider to that that Coverley could have helped her. Vestry could not have done it alone. He would have lacked the physical strength; and in Roper's experience of murder, it was a rare killer who operated in concert with another, except in a crime of passion, the classical *folie à deux* in which the lover and mistress did away with whoever stood in the way of their love, lust, or whatever.

The killing was too inept to have been planned. Ergo, it was probably what Roper had earlier thought: a Domestic. The victim knew his killer; knew him, or her, intimately. And if it was a Domestic, then the killer either lived in the house or had been a guest at that dinner party last night. Not a fact, but too probable to ignore. Then there were Winterton's keys. On the table when Faulkner had left the house. So either Winterton had gone out in the early hours of this morning, or someone had borrowed them to gain a later entry into the house, then put them in Winterton's pocket before he—or she—had thrown the body over the cliffs. And the last person to leave the house had been Jack Coverley.

And the other two guests, O'Halloran and Tasker? Could the one be disregarded because of his cloth and the other by virtue of the fact that he made his living out of the law. Bent solicitors weren't outside Roper's experience, and wayward vicars did occasionally make the Sunday newspapers.

What was also possible was that he was on the wrong track altogether, that perhaps he ought to be looking further afield than the oddly assorted coterie that had dined at Winterton's house last night. But something deep down inside him, instinct perhaps, the little voice of reason and experience, all encouraged him to pursue his present course.

But not now. It was late, and the sharp prickling behind his eyes reminded him again just how tired he was. There was nothing to do now that could not wait until tomorrow.

SOME twenty minutes before Roper had finally turned in for the night and gone home, Saul Crossways had debouched from the Mariners' Arms and into the darkness.

He took two resolute paces towards the middle of the pavement. Paused while he took his bearings and the horizon levelled off. Sniffed tentatively at the keen night air. Decided it was not to his liking and quickly lifted his muffler to cover his nose and mouth; and re-inhaled his own beery breaths which at least were warm. Slowly turned to face the west and, swaying slightly, and with one mittened hand clasping the neck of a bottle of Haig in the capacious pocket of his overcoat, set course for his doss at Monk's Cove.

It had been one of his better days. The *Argus* had forked out the modest ten pounds he had asked for, and, as well, the story he had repeated over and over in the public bar of the Mariners' had kept him in beer for the entire evening. It had been the most monumental binge he could ever remember, and in his pocket was more booze that hadn't even been touched yet.

He wove his way across the end of the jetty and struck slightly to the left to take him past the corner of the pottery. Having successfully negotiated the corner he aimed himself to the left again, passed the old Customs House, then the fish warehouse. There were other footfalls crackling on the frozen slush behind him, and from time to time voices rose and fell with that hushed heartiness that often abounds at closing time. A couple of cars passed him and lit the snow like quicksilver.

Apart from a skid or two, and a pause to relieve himself in a dark alley, he made a fairly straight line to the edge of town. As he came out on to the cliff road he was dimly aware of a clock a half mile or so behind him strike once for the quarter after eleven. It began to snow again.

WHOEVER had delivered his cash from the *Argus* had arrived in a car early that afternoon. At the time, Crossways was in his crypt, busily dismantling the cigarette ends for which he had trawled the town during the course of the morning and re-rolling the fragments of tobacco into Rizla papers. He heard a

car door slam shut. Hunched over his smoky fire at
the foot of the steps, he stilled and he listened.

Somebody coughed as the raw air caught at his
lungs. Then again, but now the visitor had drawn
closer. Crossways reached out for one of his more
substantial pieces of driftwood and took a good grip
on one end of it. His brain these days was more
often muddled than not, but not so muddled this cold
afternoon as not to recognise a possible usurpation
of his billet.

He rose, clutching his piece of wood, and tilted
an ear up the steps, ready, in his scrambled way, to
do battle with whoever the intruder might be.

But there was only silence. For a long time.

Saul Crossways stayed poised, his makeshift club
held ready.

And he waited. But nothing happened, nobody
came.

Then he heard that cough again, but more distantly; then, more distantly still, the slam of the
same car door.

He lowered the piece of driftwood. It had been a
false alarm. Then, slowly, it occurred to him,
through his alcoholic haze, that the visitor might
have been from the local newspaper, the one he had
talked to on the telephone this morning.

He waited until he heard the car engine being
started and he was sure it was moving away, then
crept up the steps and peered covertly over the top-
most one. The man from the *Argus* had brought his
money. Near the gateway, the snow on top of the
broken wall had been disturbed.

With no more thought, he hurried up the last few
steps and with the skirt of his overcoat flapping,

scurried across to the gateway and lifted the stone from beneath which protruded a corner of a new white envelope. He lifted the stone and eagerly plucked up the envelope and ripped off a corner of it between his teeth. Ten coins. What he called 'oncers'. All mint new ones.

Only then did he realise that the car he had heard had not gone, but stood a hundred yards away on the rise of the cliff road. And that whoever was driving it was watching him.

But then, with a clumsy snatching of the gears and a puff of exhaust, the car shot off and went from sight in the hollow beyond the rise. It had happened quickly. In the poor light Crossways hadn't even seen what colour it was.

AND NOW, at the day's end, apart from a fistful of coins, the ten pounds were gone; although the bottle of Haig would see him through most of tomorrow and for breakfast on the day after that, so that he wouldn't have to leave the homely fug of his doss and go out into the cold. And as for the day after that; well, that would look after itself the way it always did.

The horizon took on another queasy tilt. A few weaving paces later it righted itself, then tilted the other way. Crossways paused for a moment while it settled. Too much fresh air, he decided. Too much fresh air mixing with the booze. It wasn't good for his constitution.

He started forward again. Slippery stuff, snow was, but at least in the darkness it helped him to see his way; and not only his way but also the way of the driver of the unlit car that was tailing him and which, every once in a while, stopped and let Crossways draw ahead again, but never quite let him out of sight.

For Saul Crossways the evening had been highly profitable, a dozen or more pints of the Mariners' best bitter on the strength of his helping the police with their enquiries. At each telling, at each table, his tale was garnished a little more. He hadn't lied. Well...not a great deal. A stretching of the truth, maybe. He had, after all, found a corpse on the beach; that much was true. Equally true was the fact that he had reported the find to the coastguards, then been interviewed by the police. Within this small framework of facts Saul Crossways had woven an intricate pattern of a tale that would very soon be the death of him.

He had hinted to upwards of thirty of the Mariners' clientele that he might know even more than he was prepared to say. That the police would undoubtedly be interviewing him again. A prime witness, he was.

'Witness to what?' asked an unbeliever.

'I was there, wasn't I?'

'Where?'

'In me doss. Not a hundred yards from where it happened.'

'But did you *see* anything?'

'It's not always what you *see* is it? A bloke can hear things, can't 'e.'

'But did you hear?'

'Ah,' murmured Crossways knowingly. 'I can't tell you that, see. They told me not to.'

'Who did?' asked the unbeliever.

'The law did, didn't they?'

Saul was easy bait. The more he was teased the more he invented, and when he had exhausted his audience in the public bar he had foolishly dared to visit the saloon. His sojourn there had been brief. George Easterby, the Mariners' landlord, had spotted him after a minute or two and come apace through his counter-flap to see Crossways back to the street. The damage, however, had been done. Saul Crossways had lurched up to but the one table in the saloon and that, had he but known it, was the biggest mistake he had ever made. The second biggest had been that he had slipped back into the public bar for one more for the road; because it gave his intending killer time to make a telephone call while Crossways quaffed that last pint of bitter.

But of all this Saul Crossways was unaware. He was content, content because his brain had more or less ceased to function. His autonomic system kept his feet shuffling along in a more or less straight line and he had his bottle of Haig stashed away in his pocket to ward off any ills tomorrow might bring. He required nothing else. And as for the pain across his chest, well, that was yet another dose of indigestion. It happened sometimes. Came and went. It didn't bother him, never had.

His own shadow suddenly leapt, elongated, in front of him, drawn by the headlights of a car on the road behind him. Then they were doused and it went dark again. Lovers, he thought. Probably pulled into the layby for a bit of nookie on the way home.

He started up the rise where that car had waited this afternoon. By the time he had crested it, he was grunting for want of breath; and the pain was worse than it had ever been before. And he had to stop and lean against the signpost that warned oncoming motorists that a dangerous curve in the road lay ahead. The pain had never been like this. Not ever. It was across his chest and down his back and down his arm and he could hardly breathe for it.

He clung to the post, slowly subsiding down it because the effort of standing up, coupled with the effort of trying to haul in air, was too much for him. He scrabbled away the muffler from over his nose and mouth, thinking that might help. But it didn't.

He remembered the bottle in his pocket. Fumbled it out. But the seal was unbroken and he simply hadn't got the strength—or the will—to rake through his carrier bag for his penknife. A drop of Scotch might have helped, the way brandy was supposed to. Only it was too much trouble and everything hurt too much, and he couldn't see properly and there was a noise in his head like rushing water.

Then lights.

He'd been born lucky. Someone had seen him. Help was at hand. A lot of headlights. Six—seven—eight, all revolving, all blurred together. They stopped beside him. A car door opened and a torch shone on his face, a fierce light, close up, so that it hurt his eyes to look at it.

He tried to speak, to explain, and his mouth opened and closed but he couldn't make the words come.

A man's voice said, 'He's ill. Look at him.'

'Rubbish,' a woman's voice snapped. 'He's drunk. And put that bloody torch out before someone sees us.'

And even through the mist of pain and alcohol

Crossways recognised that these voices were not friendly. They were not the voices of anyone he knew, but through the pain percolated the idea that they knew him. That they were not here by fortuitous accident. That they were not here to help him.

'Get him in the car.' The woman.

Rough hands hauled him from the post and jerked him to a sitting position.

'God, he stinks.' The man had said that.

Pain lanced through Crossways like a hot sharp knife. Worse than before, and this time it didn't subside. He was hoisted to his feet, slung over a shoulder like a sack of barley.

'For Christ's sake hurry up,' the woman said.

Gasping for air, Crossways felt himself being carried a few paces, then unceremoniously bundled into somewhere warm. His head was jarred, a door was slammed shut, then another, then another. He was in a car and it was moving.

To where he no longer cared. Bounced agonisedly up and down he slipped into unconsciousness, surfaced briefly to feel that he was being carried like a sack again. A torch flashed.

'Hurry up!' urged the woman, and that was the last sound that Saul Crossways ever heard.

THIRTEEN

THE SHARP END of another day. The second of this new year. It had snowed again heavily during the night but now, capriciously, a thin wintry sun was shining, so that if you were inside in the warm and couldn't see the piled-up snow you could easily imagine it was early spring.

A half-hour ago, at eight o'clock, the waitress that Mrs. Fowler had hired for Winterton's dinner party had called in at the station, not quite voluntarily because it had been her father's suggestion, but of her own free will. She was on her way to work, couldn't stop long, *if* that was all right.

'Yes, Miss Butterworth. That's fine. Thoughtful of you to come in at all.'

Butterworth. Sally. Miss. 14 Bishop's Terrace. Twenty years old and saving up to get married, hence her need to do a spell of, you know…

'Moonlighting?'

'Yes. That's it.' A quick nervous smile. 'Moonlighting.' A plump, blonde, homely girl sporting an inexpensive engagement ring, and a touch in awe of her surroundings. She had never been inside a police station before, not even as far as the duty desk.

She declined Roper's offer of a cup of tea. She had not long had breakfast, but thanks all the same.

She had arrived at Westwinds House at half-past six on the evening in question. For the first half-an-hour she had helped Mrs. Fowler to finish setting the table and generally assisting in the kitchen. From seven-fifteen until eight o'clock she had helped to replenish the guests' glasses and kept an eye on the cooking. At eight-fifteen, she and Mrs. Fowler had repaired to the kitchen and shared the chores of getting the meal ready for the table. She had served dinner, mostly on her own, at eight-thirty, seen to the bulk of the washing-up and left the house at ten-thirty. On the dot, because her fiancé had come to fetch her in his car. The two of them had gone home to Bishop's Terrace, she had bathed and changed, then the two of them had gone on to a party of their own.

'Did you notice anything untoward, Miss Butterworth?'

'Like what?'

'Any hostility between any of the guests. Anything of that sort.'

She lowered her face and fiddled nervously with her new ring. 'I'm not sure I ought to say,' she said hesitantly. 'It's sort of confidential, you see—the agency, I mean. We're always being told not to talk about where we've worked. Gossip, you know.'

'Understood, Miss Butterworth.' Roper hunched confidentially closer over the desk. 'But anything you tell us is strictly between us. You. Me. The inspector here. And it's a murder, you see.'

She lifted her face and looked from one to the other of them anxiously.

'Well, I did notice *something*,' she said. 'There was a big man there. With a beard. One of the guests. I saw him get hold of Mr. Winterton. By the sleeve. Like this. You know.' She took a fistful of the sleeve of her own brown coat and screwed it up, just below the elbow. 'I thought he was going to hit him. Hit Mr. Winterton, I mean. They were standing in the hall.'

'But he didn't hit him?'

The girl shook her head.

'No. Young Mr. Winterton came out of the front room to answer the door—it was the vicar, I think, who'd come. The bearded man said something nasty to Mr. Winterton...'

'What did he say?'

'I'm sorry, I didn't hear.'

Roper smiled encouragingly. 'So how do you know that he said something nasty. Perhaps he didn't.'

The girl nodded strenuously. 'Oh, he said something *nasty,* all right. You could tell. His eyes. And he was frowning. And when he let go of old Mr. Winterton's sleeve he sort of *pushed* him away. You know?'

And that was all she had seen. She wasn't unintelligent, she had simply been kept too busy.

Mrs. Fowler had treated her well. Motherly, you know. A lot of people who hired a maid for the evening thought they were renting a drudge to do all the dirty work. But not Mrs. Fowler. A couple of times she had brought a couple of vodkas and tonics out to the kitchen. It had been New Year's Eve, after all. And to Miss Butterworth's surprise, Mrs. Fowler, at the end of the evening, had pressed a ten-pound note into her hand.

'How about Mr. Winterton? The elder one?'

Oh, he was nice too. Chatty, you know. He'd come out to the kitchen at about quarter past ten and thanked her. Not many did that, either.

It had been pointless to press her any further. Miss Butterworth was of the ilk that minded its own business and got on with its work. By eight-thirty the W.P.C. who had escorted her up from the duty desk had escorted her back down again.

WINTERTON'S MURDER had made the front pages of several national newspapers this morning; and the general public had been led to believe thereby that the investigative machinery was proceeding to a swift conclusion to the matter.

It was not. The bearings were oiled and the engines were primed, but so far as Roper was concerned the investigation was scarcely off the ground yet. A half-dozen uniformed men, armed with Xeroxed copies of Winterton's address book, were making enquiries of his other cronies and business associates who lived in the county, but Roper held out little hope in that direction. For his money, the odds were still on the bevy of oddities who had been at Westwinds House on New Year's Eve. One of them, two of them, maybe even three.

The items of evidence could be enumerated on the fingers on one hand. The fragment of cotton and nylon snagged on the walking stick; the wristwatch that had stopped at half-past five, and the bunch of keys that had lain on the half-moon table in Winterton's hall on New Year's Eve, and had been found in the pocket of Winterton's dinner jacket the next morning on the beach. On the face of it, if Faulkner had been telling the truth, it was possible that Winterton himself had picked them up on his way out to some middle-of-the-night appointment. Or Coverley had, when he had gone back to the house for his gloves. And Roper still had two fingers to spare.

'I don't go for the small hours jaunt,' said Miller. 'It was bloody cold, and he was an old man and he'd have needed a car. And according to Mrs. Fowler, he didn't drive any more.'

'Somebody might have fetched him.'

'Then somebody in the house would have heard the car.'

'Perhaps they did. And they've lied to us.'

'Why?'

'Perhaps they know who the somebody was and feel like covering up.'

Miller's face briefly registered impatience as Roper played devil's advocate.

'I know what you're thinking, son,' said Roper, propping his elbows on the desk and cupping the fist of one hand in the curved palm of the other. 'This is your patch and your murder and I'm only here to make it look like a big-time murder investigation—and make a name for myself. Right?'

'But we're not *doing* anything,' argued Miller. 'We're just *sitting* here.'

'What do you suggest then? Go out and charge somebody, do we? Saturate the town with bobbies, set up road-blocks? Door to door enquiries? Do you know what that sort of strategy *costs*? Chief Constable sees the overtime bill, I lose my pension and you finish up back on the beat. Right?' Roper dropped a hand to slide back his cuff from his wristwatch. 'It's ten to nine. The County forensic boy'll have all the cars once-overed by tonight. Postmortem's at two-thirty; with luck we'll have the pathologist's report by six this evening. Armed with

that and the results of the car checks we could have
a result before midnight. Right?'

Miller opened his mouth, but a knock at the door
cut off whatever he was going to say and he closed
it again like a goldfish.

It was the W.P.C. who had shown up Sally Butterworth earlier. She looked faintly puzzled.

'It's Mr. O'Halloran, the vicar, sir,' she said,
standing uncertainly by the edge of the half-open
door. 'And a Mrs. Fowler. They've asked if they
can have twenty minutes with you.... If you're not
busy, that is.'

'What about? Did they say?'

The W.P.C. hitched a shoulder. 'No, sir. Mr.
O'Halloran said it was a private matter, and if you
can't see him now, perhaps you could give him an
appointment for later on today.'

'No. Now's fine,' said Roper, already clearing the
desk in front of him of its litter of papers and stack-
ing them neatly to one side. 'Another chair and four
cups of tea, please, my dear. Then bring 'em up.'

THE W.P.C. held the door open and O'Halloran ushered Mrs. Fowler ahead of him into the office. She
looked decidedly ill at ease, almost as if she had
been brought here against her will. O'Halloran was
a tall, lean dark man with thinning hair and an air
of holy determination about him. Forty-five-ish and
quick to get to business once Miller had effected his
introductions to Roper.

'In short, Superintendent, Mrs. Fowler telephoned
me very early this morning to ask my advice. That
advice was that she should visit you as soon as possible and explain her circumstances to you plainly

and without prejudice to any further questions you may have to ask her. She has come here voluntarily, I hasten to add, and I have accompanied her for—shall we say—moral support. I have advised her to be frank and that is what she wishes to do. With your permission, naturally.'

Roper savoured all that unhurriedly.

'Do I take it that what you want to tell me is relevant to the death of Mr. Winterton, Mrs. Fowler?'

She shook her head. 'No. Not exactly. It's something about myself that I—and Mr. O'Halloran—think you should know about. Something you'll find out about me in the end, anyway. And if you do—and I haven't told you about it—well, it might lead you to think that I killed Mr. Winterton. Or at least cast suspicion on me.'

'I see,' said Roper, gravely. He sat back in his chair. 'With respect to Mr. O'Halloran here, are you sure you wouldn't rather tell me whatever it is in the presence of someone like a solicitor? Mr. Tasker, say? It might be wiser.'

'No,' she said. 'It's something Mr. O'Halloran already knows about, and something I'd rather not have spread around more than necessary. It's also something that I'd rather Mr. Coverley didn't know about. Not yet, anyway.'

She sat tensely on the edge of her chair, her handbag and gloves clasped tightly together on her lap. Neat, prim.

'Well, I can certainly promise not to tell Mr. Coverley,' Roper assured her. 'But if it turns out to be evidence in the case of Mr. Winterton's death, then of course it could become public. There's nothing I can do about that.'

'Yes, naturally,' she said. 'I understand that. But it bothers me that I didn't tell you the entire truth about myself yesterday. I couldn't. Not with Mr. Coverley there. You see, Mr. Winterton knew something else about me. More than my trial for the murder of Gerald Fanning, I mean.'

Roper leaned back in his chair as if he had all the time in the world.

'Right, then, Mrs. Fowler,' he said. 'I'm ready when you are.'

SHE BEGAN SLOWLY and it took her some time to gather momentum. It was a story, clearly, that she had told rarely, and it was a longer one even than Vestry's and far more tangled. From time to time Roper made a note on the pad on his knee, but neither interrupted nor prompted her.

After being cleared of Gerald Fanning's murder she had decided that she would have to make a fresh start. Somewhere far away. Somewhere far enough away for the taint of the trial in England not to have reached. She settled for South Africa on the advice of her solicitor, and arrived there in the southern spring of nineteen sixty-one. A job in those days was easy to find. The first one was in a dress-salon in the better part of Johannesburg; but she was a qualified children's nurse and selling dresses soon bored her. So she signed up with a nursing agency, which eventually found her a post down in Durban. There were two children to look after. Their father was a widower. His name was Fowler.

The Fowlers' house overlooked the sea a few

miles out of Durban itself. The children were well-behaved and no trouble, and she had the run of the house. She had fallen, as she put it, on her feet. Fowler himself was a barrister and only a second generation South African. It was the kind of job she had always dreamed about, in fact it was scarcely a job at all because so few demands were made upon her. When Fowler's housekeeper left, she took on that task as well. There was a black housemaid and a black cook, and a gardener as well, so the work still wasn't arduous.

She and Fowler grew closer together, especially at weekends. Picnics on the beach with the children, swimming in the Indian Ocean, sunbathing in the never-ending sunshine. It was heady stuff, and Fowler was an attractive man.

'We formed an attachment. Became lovers.... He asked me to marry him. I didn't want to; I was terrified of what had happened back in England catching up with me.... His being a barrister; it could have ruined his career.

'Then he suddenly discovered that he had cancer—of the stomach. The specialist told him that it was inoperable. Terminal.... I went to Cape Town with him, but it didn't do any good. We must have seen a half-dozen specialists, but they all told us the same.... A year, they said. At most. And there'd have to be drugs. Without drugs, they said, he would have even less. Six months, one told us.

'I agreed then to marry him.... I couldn't refuse, you see. Special licence. That was in Cape Town....'

For a few months, their life was as ordinary as it could be under the circumstances. Fowler carried out a few more of his professional commitments, made the practice over to his partner, then retired to enjoy the little of life that was left to him.

Roper continued to listen in silence, speculating upon her possible motive for calling in on him like this, waiting patiently for her to come to the point, wary as always of the gratuitous autobiography. Few people ever told policemen more than they had to.

In six months, Fowler's condition changed dramatically.

'He had to be put on Diamorphine…a form of heroin…a nurse came in twice a day to give him injections.

'And then he changed his will.'

Roper at last broke his silence:

'A barrister? And he waited six months before he changed it?'

'No, he'd changed it before,' said Mrs. Fowler. 'As soon as we'd come back from Cape Town. He'd made a quarter of his estate over to me, but later on he decided to make it a half—I'd promised to look after the children, you see. After he'd gone. He wanted to be sure that I was adequately provided for.'

And then, finally, Mrs. Fowler came to the point. 'He died. Six weeks after he'd revised the will.'

But that wasn't all. Mrs. Fowler's gloved fingers fiddled with the catch of her handbag. 'It was an overdose,' she said. 'Of Diamorphine.'

'How much of an overdose?' asked Roper.

'A hundred and fifty milligrams,' said Mrs. Fowler.

'And the prescribed dose?'

'Forty,' she said.

Roper resisted whistling his surprise between his teeth with commendable self-control.

'He gave it to himself, Superintendent,' she said. 'I'm sure of it.'

'Did he leave a note?'

She shook her head.

'No. There was a pad on the coverlet, and a pencil by his hand; as if he'd been going to. But either he'd mistimed giving himself the injection or the pain had simply become too unbearable.

'I don't think anyone would have thought too much of it,' she went on 'if it hadn't been for that change in his will. And, of course, that when the Durban police checked back they found out that I was Grace Dacre and that I had faced a murder charge here in England.'

'But you were cleared on that charge.'

'Oh, yes,' she said. 'I certainly was. But the *stigma* was still there, you see, and the public prosecutor made a great play of the fact that I had been indicted before. For murder, even though I was found not guilty.

'The Durban police charged me with murder,' she went on. 'And I was tried. I'd pleaded not guilty, but then my husband's doctor—who'd been called for the prosecution—suggested that my husband's pain might have been so intense that I might have been tempted to give him the overdose at his own request. My counsel thought my case was going badly—and the doctor's evidence seemed like a life-line. He asked me to reconsider my plea.' Her gaze lifted and fixed levelly on Roper. 'I stood to be hanged. So I lied. I told my counsel that what the doctor had said was true. I pleaded guilty—a mercy killing.'

'Perjury,' said Roper.

'Yes,' she said. 'I know.'

'And what did the jury say?'

'Guilty,' she said. 'But with a recommendation for clemency.'

'What did they give you?'

'Life,' she said. 'Twenty-five years.... But I only served fifteen. When I was released I was served with a deportation order.'

It was at this juncture that the welfare society eased her exit from South Africa. It paid her fare and gave her a letter of introduction to its English counterpart in London which, in turn, passed her over to the Reverend O'Halloran, and it was O'Halloran who had found her the post with Winterton.

'AND THAT'S IT?' said Roper. 'That's what you wanted to tell me?'

'It seemed important,' she said. 'I felt you ought to know. Before you found out for yourselves.'

Roper put his notepad back on the blotter. Both O'Halloran and Mrs. Fowler watched him. Miller was still jotting a few notes of his own.

'Mr. O'Halloran?'

'To the best of my knowledge, all that Mrs. Fowler has told you is true, Superintendent.'

'When Inspector Miller interviewed you yesterday, Mr. O'Halloran, you didn't think it was worthwhile to mention all this. Why was that?'

'I hold a position rather like your own, sir,' said O'Halloran. He had pale, forthright eyes, eyes so pale that they were disconcertingly at odds with his hair and complexion. But he was straight, too straight. Almost an innocent, despite his calling. 'I was unable to divulge what Mrs. Fowler has just told you without her agreement. And the Society rather frowns upon such indiscretions. Naturally, if someone in authority had written to the Society in London—with the necessary justification...'

'Yes, sir, I'm sure,' interrupted Roper.

But the Reverend O'Halloran was now in full flight. 'As Mrs. Fowler has told you, it was I who introduced her to George Winterton—as the county representative of the Society. Upon her release from prison in South Africa my opposite number in Durban contacted me. When Mrs. Fowler arrived back in England, it was I who met her at the airport. It needed only the shortest acquaintance for her to strike me as being remarkably frank. I would even go so far as to say that—having known her now for several years—I, for one, believe that she was misjudged at her trial. And my colleagues in South Africa were of a similar mind. And I know, for a fact, that Mr. Winterton voiced not one *single* complaint about her work for him. Quite the contrary, in fact. Indeed, he was loud in her praises. Several occasions...'

'Mr. O'Halloran,' Roper broke in again, but this time determinedly. 'Please, sir, I've a question.'

O'Halloran blinked. 'Oh. Yes. I'm sorry. Please.'

'Tell me, sir, did you tell Mr. Winterton about *why* Mrs. Fowler had served a term of imprisonment in South Africa?'

O'Halloran nodded gravely. 'Oh, yes. Yes, indeed. A question of trust, you see. To ask someone to take an alleged—I stress *alleged*, Superintendent—criminal into his house without relating the entire set of circumstances. That would have been a *gross* omission.'

'How did you first meet Mr. Winterton, Mr. O'Halloran? A church-goer, was he?'

'Yes. But alas, not a frequent one.'

'And yet he was a member of the parochial council.'

'Yes. He was,' agreed O'Halloran. 'A little unusual, I have to admit, but the church does have a secular side and Mr. Winterton's business acumen proved to be most useful to us. As I have already said, he gave of his time unstintingly. Unstintingly. And there are a great many self-styled Christians who do not do that, I have to say.'

'So how did you get to know him, sir? In the first instance.'

Oh—er—through Mr. Vestry. I am, the—er—college chaplain—and as you probably know Mr. Winterton was on the board of governors.'

'And you visited his house fairly often, did you, sir?'

'Often, yes. As I said before, on church business. But he *had* asked me to call back for what he called a—er—chin-wag this afternoon. Of course he was dead by then. But he had something, he said, to tell me. Something important, he led me to believe. He needed my advice. I understood that it was a matter concerning the—er—good name of the College—a potential scandal that he wished to avert...'

Roper's flagging interest was abruptly brought to life again. He and Miller both looked up like two marionettes worked by the same string.

'Really, sir? Did he give you any hint as to what this scandal might be?'

'Oh, no. Alas. I have no idea. So, whatever it was, we might never know.' O'Halloran shrugged disconsolately, making his neck briefly shrink, turtle-like, into his clerical collar.

No, thought Roper. Nobody might ever know. But it would be a fair guess that Winterton had been going to tell O'Halloran that vindictive tale of his about Clive Vestry's alleged adventure with his nephew....

'So really it was the South Africa business that Mr. Winterton was holding over your head—not the Fanning affair at all?'

'Yes,' she said. 'That's right. The last thing I wanted Jack to know was that I'd been in prison. Mr. Winterton threatened to tell him.'

'Anything else you want to tell me, Mrs. Fowler? Nothing you might have forgotten? You're sure?'

Mrs. Fowler was shaking her head. Exactly why she had come along here this morning was still not completely clear but, if it had done nothing else, her visit had cleared up the mystery of O'Halloran's reticence about her when Miller had interviewed him yesterday. For the rest, what had happened to her in South Africa might or might not be relevant to the death of George Winterton, but even if it wasn't, it was grist of some kind or another, and it wouldn't be wasted.

Roper slid back his chair, thanked them both and escorted them out to the head of the stairs. He was gone for a minute, no more, but that had been time enough for Miller to take the brief telephone call that would have Roper and himself down at Monk's Cove again as fast as a car could get them there.

FOURTEEN

ROPER MADE HIS cautious way down the snow-covered steps to the crypt.

Crossways lay spreadeagled on his face on the flagged floor with his feet towards the steps. He was capless. And quite dead.

Miller aimed his torch while Roper crouched beside the body. There was an ammoniacal stench of urine. He felt for the artery just beneath Crossways' ear. The flesh might have been ice. With surprising gentleness, Roper then lifted Crossways' head an inch from the stones and turned it towards him. The old man's nose was hideously flattened and his beard bloodied. He had been dead for a long time.

'Who found him?'

'The bobby upstairs,' said Miller. 'About half an hour ago. When he came down, he found Crossways lying here. And all that.' Miller swept the torch-beam across to the far side of the crypt. The stack of flattened cardboard boxes that had been Crossways' bed had been stripped down and flung everywhere. The hessian sack pillow had been ransacked and its stuffing of grubby rags and newspapers scattered over the floor. But why? For what? There seemed so little point to so much mayhem to so little effect. Crossways had nothing. He was a loser, one of the lesser coins of society's small change. Roper straightened up. When he had looked at Crossways' battered, grizzled face he had suffered a few mo-

ments of infinite sadness and compassion. What was
surfacing now was a cold and unreasonable anger.
This death was no less a one than George Winterton's. It wouldn't make the front pages of tomorrow's dailies but that did not diminish the outrage
of it.

'Have you checked his pockets?'

'Only the overcoat,' said Miller. 'They were
empty.'

'How about his cap? And that torch he had? And
his plastic carrier bag?'

'I've already looked. They aren't here.'

'Then find 'em. And get Harford here and somebody from the Coroner's Office and the photographer. The whole bloody shooting match.'

'Right,' said Miller.

Roper again looked down at Crossways' body,
lying there as though it had been casually tossed
from a shovel, and lifting his gaze again he pinned
the last of his wrath on the pale oval of Miller's face
simply because there was nowhere else to put it. He
said, very softly, 'I gave you an order, laddie. Do
it.'

Miller wisely said nothing, and went.

Roper surfaced to the chill fresh air and the wan
winter sunlight. The only sharply defined footprints
were those of himself, the constable who had found
Crossways, and Miller. There were a dozen others
that last night's snow had filled in and rendered
formless. Most of them had to be Crossways', but
two sets at least, one going one way and one the
other, had to belong to whoever had turned over the
old vagrant's few pathetic belongings. And, just possibly, killed him.

'Are you the chap who found him?'

'Yes, sir,' said the constable. 'Poor old sod.'

'Yes,' muttered Roper. 'Damn bloody right.'

He walked slowly away beside the path towards the two heaps of stones that had once been the abbey entrance.

Crossways had obviously been a creature of habit. Almost all of the mess of footprints lay within a band about a yard wide all the way to the gap in the stones. From there, another band of footprints took a slightly diagonal path to the cliff road. Roper tracked them as far as the verge, where they disappeared in the foot-high heap of dirty brown slush hurled aside by passing cars.

From here he could clearly see the area of cliff top where Winterton had gone over yesterday. It was possible that the two deaths were connected. It might even be a fact; but for something to be a fact required evidence to make it so, and as yet he hadn't got any.

The chill air cut like a knife. Three or four hundred yards away, where the road curved sharply, a warning sign stood blackly against the sky. In the middle distance two approaching police cars snaked over a rise and dipped out of sight again into a hollow.

CROSSWAYS' GRIMY CAP lay half-buried in the snow at the road's edge like a crushed bird. One of the young cadets had found it. A few paces away, near the warning sign that heralded the dangerous curve in the road, the curled corner of a plastic carrier bag could just be distinguished sticking up out of the snow. Roper didn't doubt for a moment that the bag had come from Woolworth's; and once uncovered would reveal a gaudy Yuletide illustration.

And there were footprints. The snow round about followed, more or less evenly and with hardly a blemish, the contours of the ground beneath. But around the post that supported the sign the snow was ploughed and scuffed, and there were several depressions that had definitely been caused by trampling feet.

It was Miller who spotted the sooty, cavernous hollow in the heaped-up snow at the edge of the carriageway a few yards further along.

'Car exhaust,' he said. 'Somebody stopped here with his engine running.' But at the time neither he nor Roper regarded the sooty gouge as being particularly significant.

The area was photographed, and Crossways' cap and carrier bag carefully excavated.

The cap was an antique. Its artificial silk lining had rotted away long since and a circle cut from a Safeways plastic bag had replaced it. A few ragged holes in the crown were large enough to put a finger through. Otherwise it revealed nothing.

The first item out of the carrier bag was an old mahogany cigar-box with a rubber-band around it. At first glance, what it contained looked like junk; a few items turned over suggested that it was Saul Crossways' lifetime collection of memorabilia. Standard-issue war medals. A '39-'45 Star, Africa Star, a yellow embroidered gerbil on a scarlet patch of material—the shoulder insignia of the Eighth Army. A clutch of cracked and faded snapshots. A group of young men in desert uniform posing proudly in front of an armoured car with palm trees in the background. Crossways could have been any one of them. A young woman, taken circa nineteen-forty if the padded shoulders of her dress were anything to go by. Another young woman. And another. And yet another. Wartime photographs; something about their hairstyles and their extraordinarily vivid lipstick and their less than successful attempts to look like Joan Crawford. A set of dice in a faded red cardboard box with frayed corners. A label in the lid gave a name and address of a shop in Marseilles. The well-used dice were made of real ivory, mellowed now to that milky yellowness of old piano keys. A broken padlock—God knows what use that had. An assortment of old keys, wartime Egyptian and Italian coins and a 9 mm Mauser cartridge-case. A cap badge of the Royal Armoured Corps, brass once, but now more verdigris than metal.

Next out of the bag was a new woollen muffler still in its cellophane wrapping, and an equally new pair of grey woollen socks still joined together with a sticky plastic label bearing their brand name. Crossways had probably picked up both during a shop-lifting expedition, but that was only of passing concern now. Last out were an army issue penknife, fork and spoon and a mug, all of which had seen better days.

It was little to show for perhaps seventy years of life.

'The bag,' said Roper. 'Did he always carry it with him?'

'From what I hear,' said Miller.

'Hear?' repeated Roper, his voice, taking on a dangerous edge again. 'This is your patch, lad. You ought to bloody well *know!*'

'Well, yes,' agreed Miller. 'Whenever I've seen him, he's been carrying a bag like that one. But I can't be sure about *always*. Sir.'

'All right then. It's all the old boy had. His worldly possessions. Right? So we'll assume the always. But even if we don't, it's safe to assume that he had it with him last night—because it's here. On the road. Right? Now, given that, what I'm asking myself is why the body is lying way over *there*— and everything the poor old bugger ever owned is lying *here*. Under six inches of snow. He wouldn't have just dumped it because it was too precious. Right?'

The constable who had excavated the carrier bag came back with another find. A bottle wrapped in off-licence tissue paper. The paper had been ripped away from the neck of the bottle. The cap-seal was unbroken. Through the couple of damp layers of paper the name 'Haig' could just be read.

'Go back to town,' said Roper. 'And try every pub and every off-licence and find out where he got it, and when and what he used for money.'

'Supposing they don't remember him?'

'Remember him?' said Roper tartly. 'I should think an old tramp with that much money would be pretty unforgettable, wouldn't you?'

CROSSWAYS had been rolled over on to his back and was bathed in the harsh glare of a portable flood-light. A chalked outline on the floor marked where he had lain.

'I'm guessing of course,' said Harford. 'But it looks as if he had a massive heart seizure. By the sound of them, there's a lot of liquid in the lungs; that's usually a sign.'

'We found some of his gear along the road. Three or four hundred yards; could he have walked that far? In the middle of a heart attack?'

Harford shook his head.

'Not impossible, but I doubt it. He wouldn't have had the breath.'

'When do you think he died?'

'I'd say an hour either side of midnight,' said Harford.

'Supposing he'd been coming down the stairs, and tripped and fallen; could he have brought on this heart attack?'

'Possible,' agreed Harford. 'But I tend to think the old chap collapsed rather than fell. If you look at his hands—' Harford crouched and took up one of Crossways' hands '—you'll see that the fingertips are undamaged. I'd say that indicated that he hadn't put out his hands to save himself. Which probably means that he was unconscious before he hit the floor.'

AND ONCE AGAIN, inevitably, there were more questions than there were ever going to be answers. Crossways, for some reason as yet unknown, had had cause to leave both his carrier bag and his bottle of whisky beside the road some distance from where his body had been found.

Why?

His doss had been searched for something. For what? And why? And when? Before he died? Or afterwards? And who would want to? Another tramp looking for easy pickings? Someone caught in the act by Crossways, and who had fled in panic when Crossways had dropped dead at his feet?

Or had Crossways come back and found the place like this? And suffered his heart seizure as a consequence?

Or, there was an alternative. That Crossways' death was linked in some way to George Winterton's. Two mysterious deaths in two days in the one town were not unlikely, but that the two bodies had been found within a couple of hundred yards of each other was very unlikely, especially when one of the victims had only yesterday found the body of the other. It was the sort of coincidence for which even a cautious bookmaker would have given astronomically high odds and still reckoned he was on pretty safe ground.

That premise took stronger root as Crossways' body was zipped into the black plastic sack and taken upstairs to the ambulance and thence to the mortuary; and all that was left of his presence was the chalked yellow outline on the damp floor and the smell of tom-cats.

The staircase darkened and a gumbooted constable ducked under the low arch of the entrance. 'Call on the radio, sir. Brady's found out where Crossways got that bottle of whisky. He bought it in the Mariners' Arms. Just before closing time last night.'

THE MARINERS' ARMS stood in the harbour wall between the heel of the jetty and the lifeboat station, and despite new licks of green and white paint looked as if it had been there for ever. In the season it did bed and breakfasts.

Easterby, its landlord, had served nearly thirty

years in the force himself before he had handed in his papers. He pulled up two pints of best bitter and brought them to where Roper was perched on a stool by the open counter-flap. It still wanted almost half an hour to official opening time.

'Skin off, Super,' he said, and almost half of his bitter went down at a swallow.

'Cheers,' said Roper.

Easterby dabbed froth off his upper lip as he put his tankard back on the counter. He was a broad, heavily-built man with a glossily bald head, the swag-belly of the committed beer drinker and the kind of eyes that looked as if they were half asleep most of the time but in fact missed very little that passed before them.

'It was about ten minutes before closing time,' he said, slowly and consideringly, as if he were trying to memorise a page or two from his notebook. 'He'd been in the public bar since nine o'clock. Bought half a pint of bitter like he always did. That was his starter. He collected a few empty glasses off the tables—one of his dodges, that. After he's done that a couple of times, the girl pulls him up another half. On the house. It's an understanding we've got between us.'

Easterby knew Crossways well. When the tramp was sober Easterby occasionally employed him to do odd jobs about the place, cleaning the brassware, sweeping out the yard. 'Nothing that needed any real savvy. But he was harmless enough, when all was said and done. And I always had a bit of sympathy for the old bugger. He was in the war, y'know. Eighth Army. In tanks. The Western Desert. Sicily, and up through Italy to Vienna. To be honest, I never knew whether to believe him or not, but I do know that he won a Military Medal. I know because I lent him a couple of quid on the strength of it; he wanted a torch for his doss. And, well, you know…' Easterby broke off coyly and took momentary cover behind his tankard.

'You don't look like a soft touch.'

Easterby shrugged hugely. 'I told you. I was sorry for him.'

'We didn't find an M.M. amongst his kit.'

'No,' said Easterby. 'You wouldn't have. I sort of took it into pawn. I've got it in the back office. You see, I figured that we all owed him a bit and, like I say, he was harmless.'

After Crossways had quaffed his second beer, he had touted himself around the public-bar tables. And last night he had seemed to be extraordinarily popular. Then the story came across the bar counter that it had been Crossways who had found the body of George Winterton on the beach that morning, and that he was also putting it about that he was the local C.I.D.'s chief witness.

'I called him over,' said Easterby. 'And had a word in his ear. Told him he'd do better to keep his trap shut in the circumstances. But ten minutes later he was doing the rounds again. So I let him get on with it. But then, about ten-fifteen, I caught him in here. In the saloon. Now that I couldn't have. As soon as I spotted him, I put him out, told him to go home—he was pretty well tight anyway. I thought he'd gone. Then, at closing time, I went in to give a hand in the public, and there he was at the counter with a fistful of pound coins. He wanted a bottle of Scotch. Haig. I remember asking him—joke, of course—where he'd nicked the money from. Two or three quid was usually his limit—and that was only on a Thursday after he'd collected his pension. I wrapped up a bottle for him, gave him his change, and he went out. Good as gold. That's the last I saw of him.'

'Did he have his carrier bag with him?'

'Was he ever without it,' replied Easterby, with a wry smile. He had pounded a beat in Redbury since soon after the war and had been the landlord of the Mariners' for the last four years; there was no time that he could remember when he had ever seen Saul Crossways without a carrier bag. 'And the bottle of Scotch was in his overcoat pocket. I saw him stuff it in there.'

'How about a torch? Black one. Rubber case. Fairly new.'

It was the one Easterby had lent Crossways the money for. Crossways had shown it to him soon after he had bought it; but, no, Easterby hadn't seen it last night. If Crossways had had it with him, it had probably been in the carrier bag.

'These customers of yours he spoke to. Can you give me a few names?'

'Good God, no,' said Easterby. 'It'd take the two of us all day.'

'How about the ones he spoke to in here, in the saloon?'

'That's easy,' said Easterby, pausing briefly to empty his tankard. 'Three of my best customers: Jack Coverley, he runs the pottery along the way here; Sam Haggerty, he's the chief reporter and general dogsbody on the local rag, and Hughie Faulkner. He owns the rag Haggerty writes for. Oh, yes, and there was one more. Short good-looking chap with iron-grey curly hair. Bit morose looking. I heard Faulkner call him Julian. About forty.'

'Yes. I know him,' said Roper. 'That would be Winterton's son. Julian.'

'Thought it might have been. Had a good reason to be morose then, didn't he.'

Easterby went away to draw up two fresh pints while Roper crossed the bar floor to the public telephone between the saloon and the billiard room. He pulled out a directory and looked up the number of the Redbury *Argus*.

HAGGERTY made himself comfortable on Miller's visitors' chair and pulled out his notebook.

'You won't want that,' said Roper. 'This time it's going to be me who asks the questions. Sorry.'

Haggerty reluctantly slipped his shorthand notebook back into his overcoat pocket. 'It's an official visit, then, is it? When you 'phoned, I thought you might have a snippet of gossip for me.'

'I have,' said Roper. 'One of your local characters. Saul Crossways. A bobby found him a couple of hours back, down at his doss. He was dead.'

'How dead?'

'We don't know yet. Could be murder.'

'Great God,' murmured Haggerty. 'You know, the longer I live on this earth, Mr. Roper, the more I realise what a shabby bloody lot the human race is.'

'You might be able to help.'

'Gladly.' Haggerty fished around his pockets for his packet of Capstan's. He offered the packet to Roper.

'No thanks. You were in the Mariners' Arms last night. Apparently Crossways came to your table and made a nuisance of himself.'

'Hardly a nuisance,' said Haggerty, through a cloud of flame and smoke as he lit a cigarette. 'Speaking for myself, I was interested to hear what he had to say. That sort of thing's my bread and butter.'

'What sort of thing?'

'From what I gathered he was helping your people with your enquiries into the death of George Winterton.'

'He said that?'

'And more,' said Haggerty. 'He was your prime witness, so he said. Knew a damn sight more than he was going to let on. The impression I got was that he might have seen old George being chucked over the cliffs. If he'd been sober, I'd have pressed him. But he wasn't, and I took most of what he said with a grain of salt.'

'You were in company,' said Roper.

'My guv'nor—Hugo Faulkner, Coverley from the pottery. And later on Julian Winterton joined us.'

'And they all heard this yarn of Crossways, I take it.'

'You couldn't miss it.'

'What time did you all leave? Can you remember?'

'We didn't so much leave as disperse,' said Haggerty. 'Coverley went back to his works—something about V.A.T. returns—before closing time that was. I went across to the toilets just after the second bell, and when I came out again Faulkner had gone. And the only one left was young Winterton. He was still at the table with a whisky in front of him. I was going to offer to drive him home, but I got the distinct feeling that he wanted to be alone. So I left him and went home myself. Not very sociable, I suppose, but I hardly knew him, you see.'

Haggerty reached for the ashtray. 'Perhaps it was kids,' he said. 'Yobbos. Followed old Saul back to the priory and did him over for the sheer hell of it.'

'So you know where his doss was. How come?'

Haggerty blew out his cheeks. 'Truth is,' he said, 'I cheated on the old chap. I took his money out of petty cash, drove round to the priory and stashed it under the prescribed chunk of masonry. I'd already half guessed who he was and that that's where he was dossing down, but I hung about to make sure. I drove about a hundred yards away and waited for Crossways to show himself. He did. I saw him come out and collect the cash.'

'Did you tell anybody? Faulkner?'

Haggerty looked pained. 'No,' he said. 'Not even Faulkner. I've got a reputation, such as it is. I'm like you people. Once I get a good source, I keep it to myself.'

'How about Crossways? Last night. Did he let on then about the priory?'

Haggerty nodded. 'Yes. He did.'

'You say you were thinking of driving Julian Winterton home. That means he must have walked to the Mariners' in the first place. A fair hike, that, wouldn't you say?'

'I think he came out in the first place to get away from Westwinds for a couple of hours. He looked pretty shattered. A bit fazed. You know? I think he came into the Mariners' for a quiet dram. When

Faulkner went to the counter to bring him into our school, he didn't look overly keen. He didn't say much when he'd joined us, either. Like he was holding a private wake, you might say.'

'How did he react when Crossways told you his little tale?'

'He didn't really get a chance to react. Coverley told Crossways to shove off. Sharpish. And in no uncertain terms, as they say.'

'How about Faulkner?'

'He was all ears,' said Haggerty. 'But then he would be, wouldn't he? He's a newspaper man. Except that with Julian Winterton sitting with us, it would have been a bit insensitive of him to do anything else but agree with Coverley and tell Crossways to make himself scarce.'

'And did he? Make himself scarce?'

'No. Not immediately. Coverley got uptight and threatened to throw him out. But then Easterby came out from behind the bar and put Crossways out in the street.'

'Coverley got uptight?'

'Angry.'

'Yes, I know what it means, Mr. Haggerty,' said Roper testily. 'I want to know how he got uptight. Sheer bad temper? Or might he have been worried about what he was hearing?'

'I wouldn't know,' said Haggerty. But then, after a second or two, the real implication of the question dawned on him and he said, 'And even if I did, it wouldn't exactly be gilt-edged evidence, would it? Jack Coverley might be a tough nut, but I doubt he's a murderer. That's for what it's worth of course.'

Roper took Haggerty back over it all again. Haggerty was an observant man by the nature of his trade and he did fill in a few more details. But nothing relevant. The last time he had seen Saul Crossways was when the Mariners' landlord led Crossways out to the street at twenty-past ten last night.

'And if you think Coverley killed Winterton, Superintendent,' he said, as he rose to leave, 'you're on a hiding to nothing. Take my word for it.'

FIFTEEN

THE STEADY THUD of printing machines came faintly through the floor of Hugo Faulkner's well-appointed office above the *Argus* works. He had left the Mariners' Arms last night a few minutes after half-past ten.

'Then I called in here to check that today's edition was running to time. Spent a couple of minutes down in the shop with my foreman, then came up here to the office to see to some paperwork. To the best of my memory I left here at about five to eleven. Got home at about ten-past.'

'And your wife could verify that?'

'Afraid not,' said Faulkner. 'But Mrs. Fowler rang me at home soon after I arrived. You can always check with her.'

'Why did she ring? Any reason in particular?'

'She was trying to track down Jack Coverley,' replied Faulkner. 'She'd apparently tried to contact him at home, then at the pottery. Then at my place. She knows that Jack and I often have a bevvy together.'

'But Mr. Coverley wasn't there?'

'No,' said Faulkner. 'I'd last seen him at the Mariners' Arms.'

'Did she say what she wanted with him?'

'No,' said Faulkner. 'She didn't say and I didn't ask.'

His memories of Crossways' prattlings in the

Mariners' last night were much the same as Haggerty's.

'I got the impression that Crossways was helping your people.... And of course the old fool was in the business of scrounging drinks. I told him to belt up and go away, so did Jack Coverley. But Crossways didn't take any notice. I think if Easterby hadn't slung him out when he did, Jack Coverley would have done it himself. I mean Julian Winterton was sitting right there with us. Couldn't have that, could we?'

'Did you get the impression he was speaking the truth? Or did you think he was simply drunk?'

'Both,' said Faulkner.

'You said just now that your wife couldn't verify the time you got home last night, Mr. Faulkner. Why was that?'

'Because I got home before she did.'

Mrs. Faulkner had arrived home round about midnight. The friend with whom she had spent the evening had apparently had some trouble getting her car started when she and Mrs. Faulkner had left the restaurant where they had had a late dinner. The friend had eventually telephoned the A.A.

Faulkner had no objections to his car being examined.

'So long as I get a good story out of all this,' he joked affably. 'I don't give a tinker's. But you won't find anything interesting in it except an ashtray full of dog-ends.'

IT WAS ONE-THIRTY by the time they drove into the loading yard of the pottery. The two forensic technicians had just arrived, and Coverley and the uni-

formed sergeant who was carrying a search warrant
were already engaged in a noisy altercation at the
foot of the iron staircase that led up to the pottery's
offices.

At the sight of Roper and Miller stepping out of
the car, Coverley came storming across and planted
himself squarely in front of them. 'I demand to
know what the hell's going on,' he said.

'They've got a warrant, Mr. Coverley. Perhaps
you haven't given them a chance to show it to you
yet.'

'Show it!' raged Coverley. He turned and flung
out one outraged finger towards the sergeant. 'That
one—that one practically stuffed the thing up my
bloody nostrils! And refused pointblank to tell me
what he was looking for.'

'It depends on what you're frightened of them
finding, Mr. Coverley,' said Roper. And when Coverley made no reply, Roper said: 'Give my lads the
keys, Mr. Coverley and let's go to your office, shall
we?'

It looked for a few seconds as if Coverley was
going to do battle, but then with graceless reluctance
he brought out his car keys and tossed them to the
sergeant. Then with a gruffly muttered, 'Upstairs,'
he turned away and crossed the yard to the iron staircase. His office opened directly on to the gridded
landing at the top. Unlike Faulkner's, Coverley's office was furnished with only the bare necessities: a
carpet, desk, filing cabinets and a couple of visitors'
chairs, although one wall was fitted along its entire
length with a glass-fronted display cabinet filled
with the pottery's colourful artefacts. On the opposite wall was a large, faded sepia photograph of the

pottery at the turn of the century with a horse and dray in front of the gates.

Coverley went behind his desk and sat on the window ledge and belligerently folded his arms. 'Right,' he said. 'Now what's this all about?'

'Did you know a character called Saul Crossways, Mr. Coverley?'

Coverley scowled. 'No. Not exactly.'

'But you did speak to him last night in the Mariners' Arms. So we're told.'

'Yes, I did,' said Coverley. 'He tried to butt in where he wasn't wanted and I choked him off. What about it?'

'The old fellow's dead, Mr. Coverley. He died soon after he left the Mariners' Arms last night.'

There was a short silence. Then Coverley lifted one shoulder dismissively and said, 'I'm sorry, of course. But what the hell is that to do with me? Last night was the first time I'd even spoken to him.'

'What time did you leave the Mariners' last night, Mr. Coverley?'

'The first bell rang just as I was going out of the door. So it would have been about twenty-past ten.'

'And what did you do?'

'I came up here,' said Coverley. 'My quarterly accounting is just coming up and I wanted to sort out my V.A.T. returns.'

'So you arrived here at about what time?'

'I didn't exactly look at my watch. But about three minutes after I left the Mariners'.'

'Did anyone see you come in here?'

'I doubt it,' said Coverley. 'I came up the outside stairs. The ones we used just now.'

'You usually come in that way, do you?'

'Yes. I always come and go that way at night. It saves the rigmarole of re-setting the security alarms.'

'But you've no proof, in fact, that you were actually on the premises, have you, Mr. Coverley.'

'No, not exactly,' said Coverley. 'Except that Mrs. Fowler rang me here at about eleven-fifteen.' Then Coverley drew his chair away from his desk and dropped into it with the weary air of a man who feels that he has restrained his natural impatience for far too long. 'Right,' he said. 'That's it. I've just about had it up to here with you people. Yesterday you practically suggested I killed George Winterton; now you're here again asking me questions because some local misfit has probably got no more than he asked for. Before last night I'd never spoken to the man. And you've got two of your men downstairs running a fine-toothed comb through my bloody car for no good reason that I can possibly think of. Just what the hell right have you got to do that?'

'We've got every right, Mr. Coverley,' said Roper. 'From what we know, Mr. Winterton's body was taken from where he was killed and dumped at Monk's Cove. That means it was either carried or taken by car.'

'Not in my damned car, it wasn't.'

'In which case you've nothing to worry about, Mr. Coverley. The two men downstairs will eliminate your car from their list. Right?'

A brisk thud of footsteps clumped up the iron staircase outside, there was a rap on the door and a uniformed constable strode in breathlessly. 'We've just found these, sir,' he said. 'And this.'

These were a pair of cotton-backed driving gloves, and *this* was a black rubberised torch.

THE CONSTABLE had brought the cold from outside in with him on his raincoat. The entire office felt suddenly chill. Roper recognised him as one of the team left down at the cliff road that morning.

'Where?'

'The gloves—about ten yards from Crossways' doss, on the path. The torch, just inside the priory gateway. We were raking through the snow.'

Both the gloves and the torch were in polythene envelopes. Both were damp and the insides of the envelopes were misted with condensation. Roper carefully drew out all three items and laid them on Coverley's desk.

Straight-faced enough from without, Roper was human enough to feel a little frisson of triumph within as he turned over the top glove to reveal its palm.

Where the knitted cotton at the base of the thumb was stitched to the damp leather there was a hole. *The* hole. No mistake.

Nor did his disappointment show when he saw how old and scarred the rubber casing of the torch was. Crossways' torch had been brand spanking new. Roper had seen it, used it. No mistake there either. More was the pity.

But still…

'Well, Mr. Coverley?' he said grimly. 'What about it?'

Coverley had lost his assurance. He leaned forward across the desk and picked up one of the gloves by its wristband, turned it inside out.

'Christ,' he muttered. Then looking up incredulously at Roper he said: 'These are mine.... The ones I chucked in the back of the car.'

'How do you know?'

Coverley lifted up the manufacturer's label on the wristband. On the back of it was a smudged and faded letter 'C' written with an indelible pencil.

'I put that mark there myself. The other one's the same. Look.'

And the other glove was indeed similarly marked.

'And you didn't go anywhere near Monk's Cove last night?'

'No,' said Coverley. 'What the hell would I want to go up there for?'

'I don't know, Mr. Coverley,' said Roper equably. 'You tell me.'

'I didn't,' said Coverley.

Coverley was, at last, deflated. He had just talked himself into a load of trouble and there was no way now of talking himself out of it. His eyes went from Roper to Miller, to the constable who had brought the gloves. If it was sympathy or brotherly understanding he was looking for, he failed signally to find it in any of them. 'And the torch is mine, too,' he said.

And that, really, was more than Roper had dared to hope for. Nigh on a confession.

'Yours, Mr. Coverley? You're sure? No, don't touch it. Just look at it.'

Coverley's hand drew back from the torch as if it had suddenly caught fire and burned his fingers.

'Take a good look though, Mr. Coverley.'

Coverley spread his hands tiredly in what was almost a gesture of surrender.

'I don't have to,' he said. 'There's a nick out of the rubber at the base of the battery compartment. It's mine all right.'

The V-shaped nick in the rubber was deep enough to reveal the metal beneath. A trace of rust, too, so the damage wasn't recent.

And when Roper asked him again, Coverley made no bones about it. The torch, as well as the gloves, were, he insisted, his. Without a doubt. But he could have sworn that his torch had been in the glove compartment of his car this morning. He was equally insistent about that.

Roper said to the constable: 'Go down and see if the forensic boys have come across a torch in that Volvo. If they have bring it up.'

While the constable was gone, Roper carefully picked up one of the gloves. On its palm was a smeary deposit of black dust that felt, to the touch, like grease. It was a curious dust, very black, very fine, and felt like grease because of the dampness of the leather. There were patches of it, too, on each fingertip.

Coverley didn't know how it had got there. The gloves were old, the last time he had seen them they had been pretty grubby; but certainly not filthy like they were now.

'Why would that be, Mr. Coverley?'

'I don't know.'

'A pair of gloves found near the bell tower; that torch close to the gateway. You really are in dead trouble, Mr. Coverley. In fact, I'd say I could arrest you on suspicion of murder right now, wouldn't you? On the other hand, any kind of reasonable explanation just might get you off the hook.'

'I don't have any explanation,' said Coverley. 'You'll just have to work it out for yourself. Sorry.'

And Roper, watching him closely, decided that things might not be all that they seemed. There was usually a pattern to these situations; if the suspect was the guilty party he or she either broke down and confessed or blundered from one lying statement to another until they tied themselves up in their own knots. Coverley was doing neither.

Roper sat down and spread his feet wide and generally made himself at home. Then he said patiently:

'Let's try again, Mr. Coverley. One last time. Shall we?'

'...But I've told you about that. I made him a partner.'

'But you didn't want him as a partner. You told us that too.'

'Right,' said Coverley. 'But do you think I'd have killed him for *that*? For *that!*'

'You tell us, Mr. Coverley. Did you?'

Coverley had got his second wind and was on the offensive again. Roper had harried him with a fusillade of questions, pushed him into one corner after another, but only to have Coverley elude him.

The telephone rang at Coverley's elbow. Angrily, he snatched it up. 'No calls,' he snapped. 'I'm busy.' Then he paused, 'Oh, it's you, Grace.' Listening, his voice, mood and attitude softened abruptly and he cupped the receiver closer. He glanced across at Roper. 'Yes,' he said, 'I've got them here, too. Have

they, by God? Have they got a warrant? Yes. That's
what they're doing here.'

A blurred silhouette fell across the wire-meshed
glass of the door to the outside stairs. A token rap
on the glass was followed by the almost precipitous
entry of the constable who had brought the gloves
and the torch from Monk's Cove.

'Sorry I've been so long, sir,' he said. 'But the
forensic lads insisted on checking it for fingerprints.'
And so saying, presenting it like a prize, he handed
Roper another torch in a plastic bag.

'Where was it?'

'Where he said. In his glove compartment.'

ROPER WAITED for Coverley to finish his conversation with Mrs. Fowler, and slam down the receiver
in the same irate manner as he had snatched it up a
few minutes earlier.

'Christ,' he said. 'You really are bloody terrorists,
you people. What the hell would you want Grace
Fowler's fingerprints for?'

'For the same reason we shall shortly want yours,
Mr. Coverley,' Roper said, lifting the second torch
from his lap and carefully putting it on the desk in
front of Coverley. 'Try that for size, will you?'

Coverley leaned forward a fraction. He gave the
torch one scathing, cursory glance, and dismissed it
out of hand. 'Not mine.'

'It was in your car. In the glove compartment.
Downstairs in your yard.'

'It's still not mine.'

Roper drew the torch back across the desk. 'No,'
he agreed. 'But supposing I told you that the last

time I saw this particular torch, it came out of Saul Crossways' carrier bag.'

COVERLEY had slumped forward in his chair and was staring gloomily down at his clasped hands hanging between his knees. 'I really don't know how it got there,' he said. 'I don't have a single bloody idea. When I saw it this morning, it didn't even remotely occur to me that it wasn't mine. You'll just have to believe me.'

And Roper almost did believe him. But there were still more avenues to explore and any one of them might yet lead back to Coverley.

Roper shrugged and turned back again to look out of the window. Down in the yard the seats of Coverley's Volvo were being gone over with a small vacuum cleaner.

'Tell me, Mr. Coverley, did Winterton himself ever mention to you that he had this hold over Mrs. Fowler? I mean, did he ever come out into the open with it? And make any threat to you? You personally, I mean.'

Coverley rocked his hanging head from side to side. 'No. Not exactly. Not to me personally.'

'So you only knew about it second hand from Mrs. Fowler?'

'Hardly second hand,' said Coverley. 'I'd had sufficient experience of Winterton's business methods on my own account. Remember?'

'But the fact that Winterton was blackmailing Mrs. Fowler was still only hearsay as far as you were concerned,' Roper insisted. 'Either Winterton mentioned it to you, or he didn't. So which was it, Mr. Coverley?'

Coverley continued to stare down with bowed head and stayed silent; evidence enough of what his answer would have been had he spoken it.

Roper said:

'When you told him you wanted an appointment with him, did you tell him the reason?'

'Oh, he damn well knew the reason all right,' replied Coverley, 'That's why he hedged about seeing me.'

'So you only *assumed* that he knew the reason. You only *ever* assumed.'

Coverley sprawled back tiredly in the chair. 'Yes,' he admitted wearily. 'I only *assumed* that he knew the reason.'

Roper cast one last net.

'Then I'll put this to you, Mr. Coverley,' he said. 'Because you thought that Winterton was putting you off, you lost your temper. You'd tried to have a word with him earlier that evening, and failed; and you had no more luck when you tried to fix up an appointment with him for later on that day. Somehow, you got hold of the keys that he kept on the hall table while you were talking to him that second time, and you returned to the house later and killed him.'

'And then I drove his body down to Monk's Cove in the middle of the night and chucked it over the cliff,' sneered Coverley. 'That's cod's wallop and you know it. You haven't got me figured at all, have you? Okay, so I've got a foul temper; but that's as far as it goes. What you're talking about is an act of murder contemplated for a couple of hours before it was carried out. I'm not like that. All I ever let go is my mouth. These,' Coverley held up his large powerful hands, 'these I keep for making pots. And those things,' he flicked a glance down at the torch and the gloves, 'if I'd killed either Winterton or that tramp, believe me, you wouldn't have found them in my car. I wouldn't have been that stupid.'

'The other guests all say that they saw the keys as they were leaving the house.'

'Well, I didn't,' said Coverley sullenly. 'Sorry.'

'Mr. Faulkner tells us they were on the table when he left the house. He would have been the last to leave; except that you went back—which you admit having done. You could have taken the keys then.'

'Except that I didn't.'

'But the keys weren't there after you'd gone. How would you explain that?'

Coverley only shrugged. 'I can't,' he said.

ROPER TUGGED on his gloves as he and Miller descended the iron stairs to the yard, aware of Coverley watching them from his office window. A Coverley still bemused and bewildered that he wasn't going down the stairs between them.

That he had been left behind was thanks to that gut reaction of Roper's. What had nagged at him, like a hollow tooth, since the finding of Crossway's body was that both Winterton's death and Crossways' death had *looked* like killings from the very beginning. In neither case had the murderer—or murderess—used his, her, or their, imagination to direct the police into suspecting suicide, or misadventure, or whatever. And it was almost as if the neglect was not neglect at all, but a deliberate trail-

ing of the bait through the tall grass to provide a
scent for the dogs to sniff at.

And what else at the end of that false trail but a
false quarry. Like Coverley.

SIXTEEN

ROPER continued to theorise in silence as Miller drove them through the slushy snow to Westwinds House. It was coming up for two-thirty in the afternoon.

They had looked like murders. They had looked like murders because they were meant to look like murders. That walking stick. Why had he, her, they, bothered to add that detail in the first place? Except to make it look as if Winterton had left his house of his own accord—which he probably hadn't. At least, not dressed the way he had been found on the beach. No scarf, cardboard-thin soles on his shoes. It didn't fit together. Any more than did the circumstances surrounding the death of Saul Crossways. If his doss hadn't been turned over it might have been assumed that he had simply collapsed with a dicky ticker. Why would anyone bother to investigate the death of a dyed in the wool wino? He didn't matter. He was a social misfit, a bloody old scrounger who hadn't had a wash in God knows how long.

But no. Somebody had scattered clues as plainly as a class of schoolboys running hare and hounds littered their trail with scraps of paper. And as messily.

Crossways' body in one place, his tatty carrier bag in another, his torch in Coverley's car. That bottle of whisky, its neat spiral of paper wrapping ripped but the metal cap still with its seal unbroken.

As if Crossways had suffered the onset of his heart attack and had been going to take down a slug of Scotch for medicinal purposes and hadn't quite had the strength to broach the bottle. Conjecture. But a lot of a copper's work was, and a good jack's conjecture was more often right than not.

Somebody in that pub last night had killed Crossways. Roper was prepared to bet his pension on it. Long established theory had it that most victims of murder either know their killer or are in some way responsible for their own sudden demise. Crossways was. Crossways was a classic victim. He had got himself fiddler's-bitch tight and shot off his mouth. That what he told his listeners was fiction was neither here nor there. That his story had been even remotely plausible to one of his listeners had been enough. Ergo: Saul Crossways had courted his own end. And that was more than conjecture. One or two new scraps of evidence would make it a hard and fast fact.

ROPER SLITHERED and skidded down the slush-clad concrete incline to the double garage at Westwinds House. Inside it, working under the fierce white light from a pair of portable butane floodlights, two more forensic technicians were checking over a Jaguar HSE with current registration plates. One was dusting the chrome door handles with charcoal powder while the other was painstakingly quartering the carpet in front of the rear seats with a magnifying glass and a pair of tweezers. At the far end of the garage was a domestic freezer, and on the wall above it a telephone, obviously the one that connected to the one in the hall of the house. A few gardening implements hung about the walls and there was a businesslike motor mower taking up the other corner near the freezer.

'Any luck?' asked Roper.

The technician working on the Jaguar's door handles straightened up. 'Not so far,' he said. 'And that one,' he pointed disdainfully with his dusting brush to the car standing next to the Jaguar, 'that's going to be a real dead loss.'

The second car was a smart little Fiat hatchback. It was waxed and polished to a showroom glitter. It looked brand new, and it needed a look at the registration plate to reveal that it was three years old. The only blemishes on its white paintwork were mud splashes along the sills and the bottoms of the doors. The remainder was immaculate.

'The inside's like it too,' said the technician. 'She had the whole bloody shot valeted yesterday in Bournemouth. Inside and out.'

'She?'

'The housekeeper. Mrs. Fowler.'

The Fiat was George Winterton's, the Jaguar Julian's.

Roper slowly circled the Fiat. There were patches of damp under each of the tyres—but so there were under the tyres of the Jaguar.

'Did she say why she chose yesterday to have it done?'

'Her guv'nor told her to. So she said.'

'It's been out. Recently.'

'They both have,' said the technician. 'Young Mr. Winterton took his out to get a new tyre fitted. And Mrs. Fowler took the Fiat into town this morning to get some groceries in. Said she had to because young Mr. and Mrs. Winterton are staying over for a few more days.'

It sounded plausible enough. But then so had most of the stories he had been told so far, even though some of them had to be downright lies.

'If you find anything, let me know. I'll be in the house.'

'Right.'

GLENDA WINTERTON showed them into the study. Her husband was sitting in the captain's chair behind the desk. There was a writing-pad in front of him and a pile of addressed envelopes at his right elbow. At his other side was a leather-bound address book, weighted open by the brass desk tidy; the handwriting in it looked like his father's.

Roper put out a staying hand as Glenda Winterton went to go back out to the hall.

'And you can stay if you would, Mrs. Winterton.'

'I need a drink,' she said. 'Do you mind?'

Close to, Roper thought he could smell gin on her breath. He wondered if she might be an alcoholic.

'And I'd rather you stayed, madam. Please.'

They stood perfectly still, like two fencers each waiting for the other to drop his guard, then finally she turned away and took up a position with her back to the window and folded her arms. At three o'clock of the afternoon it was already twilight outside.

'Another address book, sir?'

'My father's business one,' said Winterton. 'Mrs. Fowler had it upstairs. She thought it might be a good idea if I wrote a few letters telling the more important people about his death.'

'I imagine they'd know by now, wouldn't they,' muttered his wife. 'It's in all the bloody newspapers, isn't it.'

Roper ignored her.

'You were in the Mariners' Arms last night, Mr. Winterton. That right?'

'Yes. I was.' Winterton drew back from the desk lamp so that his face went into the shadows and only his eyes caught the light from it like two dull beads. 'But I don't understand. My father was already dead by then.'

'What did you do afterwards?'

'I left at closing time and came back here.'

'How, sir?'

'I walked,' said Winterton.

'And you got back here to the house when?'

'About ten-past eleven.'

'And you walked.'

'I'd left the car here, so I had to.'

'Is that right, Mrs. Winterton? Your husband arrived back here last night at ten-past eleven?'

'It seems about right.'

'Seems?'

'I was in bed and asleep, for Christ's sake.'

'Look,' Winterton broke in. 'Last night. I needed fresh air and I went for a walk. I wound up down at the harbour and I needed a drink so I called in at the Mariners'. I can prove I was there. Faulkner will vouch for me, and a chap called Haggerty, and that potter chap.'

'There was one of the local characters there too, a tramp. Crossways, Saul Crossways. I understand he tried to join you and your friends.'

'Oh, yes,' sighed Winterton deprecatingly. 'That

old fool. He was about all I wanted last night, the bloody old ghoul. Coverley sent him packing, thank God.'

Roper said: 'That old fool as you call him is dead, Mr. Winterton. And was very probably murdered, like your father.'

'Then I'm sorry,' said Winterton. 'But that's not my fault, is it?'

'When you left the Mariners', you walked straight home?'

'Yes. I told you.'

'Anyone see you? Did you have to stop and ask anyone the way?'

'I'm sure *dozens* of people saw me. But they probably wouldn't know me from Adam. And I knew the way back.'

'Did you go out again? After you got home?'

'No.'

'Mrs. Winterton?'

'I don't think he did.'

'But you're not sure?'

'Look,' she admitted. 'I was down here on my own last night and I'd had more than a few drinks. Boredom. You know?'

'So you don't really know what time your husband came home last night, or if he went out again?'

She had the grace to look uncomfortable. 'No, I don't,' she said. 'Not exactly. But I'm pretty certain he didn't go out again once he came to bed.'

'Well, thank you for your frankness, Mrs. Winterton,' said Roper. 'And you say that you were down here yesterday evening on your own. Does that mean Mrs. Fowler was out as well?'

'No, she was in all evening. Upstairs in her flat.

I heard her television going. And her sewing machine.'

'All evening?'

'Certainly, until I fell asleep.'

'That's right,' Julian Winterton interrupted. 'The television was still going up there when I got back from the Mariners'. It went off at about half-eleven and I heard her running a bath.'

'You're sure, sir?'

'Of course I'm bloody sure.'

So alibi upon alibi, or lie upon lie. There was no way of telling.

Roper changed his tack. 'What do you know about your father's will, sir?'

'I've already told you. I don't figure in it.'

'Why, sir? Do you know?'

'I presumed I'd dropped a black of some sort.'

'Like what?'

'Oh, tell them for pity's sake,' his wife cut in. 'What the hell does it matter? They're bound to find out in the end, aren't they? Like ferrets down a bloody rabbit hole, these two.'

Winterton's face advanced again into the pool of light from the desk lamp. He clasped his hands together on the writing pad, and Roper waited patiently for yet another revelation. They're bound to find out in the end anyway; he'd lost count of how many times he had heard that cry, or subtle variations of it during the course of the last couple of days.

'I should have told you yesterday, Superintendent,' said Winterton at last. 'Stupid not to have. I'm sorry.... But, you see, I don't have any rights here. None at all. Not legally speaking. When my mother died, some fifteen years ago, she left me everything she owned and that her husband could not possibly lay a claim to. It wasn't a great deal, a few thousand pounds, worth more in those days, of course. But it was enough for me to set up my business, enough to keep body and soul together for a year if it all fell through.'

'Did your father cut you out of his will because of that?'

'He wasn't my father, Superintendent,' said Winterton. 'That's the point. Attached to my mother's will was a letter to my father—or, rather, the man I supposed to be my father. It stated that he was not my father—with sufficient evidence to prove it. Towards the end, she grew to hate him, you see. And that was her own way of getting back at him. He checked back the dates she'd written in the letter, and found out that she had to be right. And that's it. He took it out on me by cutting me out of his will, told me he wasn't leaving all he'd worked for for somebody else's bastard to grow fat on. End of story.'

'And yet he invited you here for Christmas, sir,' said Roper. 'And you came.'

'I've never been able to bear a grudge, Superintendent,' said Winterton. 'And he did see me through the first twenty years of my life. And in a way we were both tricked, weren't we? Both of us.'

'You're too soft, Julian,' Glenda Winterton broke in pithily from her shadowed sentry box by the window. 'You always have been.'

Her husband glared up angrily at her. 'All right, Glenda,' he said. 'Now it's your turn. You'd better tell them about that page you tore out of the family Bible.'

'It isn't important,' she retorted. 'It doesn't have any bearing on anything.'

'I'll be the judge of that, madam,' said Roper. The page torn from the Winterton's family Bible had not exactly been troubling him, but like a hole in the road it was there, and better filled in than skirted. 'Did you tear it out?'

'Yes, I did… The old man had obliterated Julian's name and written 'bastard' beside it. Wouldn't *you* have torn it out?'

'But your husband's told us you haven't been here in years, Mrs. Winterton; how did you know that Mr. Winterton had crossed your husband's name out.'

'Curiosity,' she said. 'I looked. I knew Julian's name was in there because the old man showed it to me the day we got married. I was interested to see if his name was still there. When I saw what he'd done, I ripped the page out. I tore it out on Christmas Eve afternoon. And I told Julian after you'd left here yesterday. He didn't know before.'

Strange pair. Strange story. Strange family. It never ceased to amaze Roper how diverse and bizarre the human race could be once it put its collective mind to it.

No, Mrs. Fowler confirmed, in the lounge after Glenda Winterton had gone upstairs to fetch her from her quarters, she had been in all evening yesterday, and all night too, come to that. There was a lot to do now that Mr. Winterton was dead. She was even thinking of moving out.

'Moving out, Mrs. Fowler?'

'It's something I have to contemplate,' she said, sitting in the armchair in front of the window and screwing a handkerchief into a rope between her nervously working hands. 'I mean I can't take it for granted in the circumstances, can I? That I'm staying on here. And I don't think I want to stay, either—in the light of what's happened.'

'But Mr. Winterton may have left you this house, Mrs. Fowler,' Roper suggested, hoping to draw her out about her knowledge of George Winterton's will. 'It isn't impossible, is it?'

'Oh, I don't think so,' she said. 'That sort of thing only happens in books, doesn't it?'

'Tell me again what you did last night, Mrs. Fowler. Whatever you remember. If it was only to go downstairs to make yourself a cup of tea. Anything.'

And she went over it all again. She had cooked a small meal for herself soon after seven o'clock. Eaten it up in her quarters and watched the television. Till eight, or thereabouts. Then she had gone downstairs to wash the dishes and put them away. On her way upstairs, she had called in on Glenda Winterton to see if she had wanted anything. She had not. On upstairs then to finish a dress she was sewing together and half watch a film on the television.

'You implied that Mrs. Winterton was on her own,' said Roper, backtracking.

'Yes, she was. She was in the lounge watching television and Mr. Winterton—I think—was in the study. Sorting out his father's papers, I think.'

'But he did eventually go out, didn't he?'

'Yes. —I heard the front door slam. About half-past nine.'

'Slam?'

'Yes,' she said. She let the rope of handkerchief slowly untwist itself. 'I think that Mr. and Mrs. Winterton might have quarrelled. I heard them shouting.'

She had no idea what it was about, but it had definitely been a slanging match.

'Then what?'

'I went back to my flat and watched the news on television. Did some more sewing. Had a bath. Went to bed.'

'You've forgotten something.'

She frowned. 'No. I'm sure I haven't.'

'Two telephone calls. At least.'

'In, you mean?'

'No,' said Roper. 'Out. You 'phoned out.'

Not for the first time, Roper thought what an attractive woman she was. Fanning the M.P. had taken up with her, then the South African Mr. Fowler, and these days Jack Coverley. So why not George Winterton? When it came to a good face and a shapely pair of legs there was no fool like an old one when it came to the crunch....

'Yes. I did. I'd forgotten. I rang Jack—Mr. Coverley—at the pottery.'

'When?'

'I don't remember.'

'Try,' said Roper.

'I can't remember.... Eleven o'clock.... Something like that.'

'Closer. Try.'

'Eleven. A minute either way. I *am* sure.'

But Coverley had not been at the pottery. She rang him again at five-past, and still got no answer.

'So I rang Mr. Faulkner—at home—to see if Jack was there. He did go there sometimes. They're friends, you see.'

'It was something urgent, was it? This call you tried to make to Mr. Coverley?'

'No,' she said. 'No. Not really. I just needed to talk to somebody. Anybody would have done, quite frankly. I was feeling low. Depressed, you know?'

Roper decelerated. 'I'm sorry to press you, Mrs. Fowler. But it's all important. Knowing where everybody was.... I take it you asked Mr. Faulkner where Mr. Coverley was? Did he know?'

'No. He said the last time he'd seen Jack was on the corner by the pottery. He gave him a toot on his car hooter. Soon after closing time. He'd assumed Jack had gone back to work. He often did. Late at night.'

'Did you ring Mr. Coverley again? After you'd spoken to Mr. Faulkner.'

'Yes, I did.'

'And was he there? Did he answer?'

'Yes. He said he'd been there since leaving the Mariners' Arms. He'd been working down on the oven and hadn't heard the 'phone ringing.'

'Time, Mrs. Fowler? It's important.'

But she could not remember. Some time between quarter and half-past eleven. Roper pushed her hard but anything closer, she said, could only be a guess.

'I really don't remember,' she said tiredly. 'Really, really, really.'

And, reluctantly, Roper had to settle for that.

THE PATHOLOGIST worked deftly, needle in, needle out, thrusting it in again as he crudely stitched up the clavicle to navel slit in Winterton's cadaver and closed off some of the stench. Across the room, the lugubrious boy, masked and gowned and rubber-booted, was bottling up a liver.

'Who the hell are you?'

'Roper, sir.' Roper held his identity card out where the pathologist could see it and still carry on with his stitching. 'Superintendent. County C.I.D.'

'Ah. Sorry. Wilson. How do. Your case is this, Superintendent?'

'Yes, sir.'

Plastic-sheathed fingers eased in a strip of blue-red stomach muscle and pinched the flesh together over the top and stitched the lips together.

'Can't tell you a great deal yet, of course. Male. White. Middle seventies. Weight a little over fifty kilos—eight stone. Fit—considering. A smoker—moderately. Last meal beef, sprouts, roast potatoes, and apple pie—with either cream or ice-cream. —Ah, that interests you, I see.'

'We usually have to wait for that information from the path. lab. You seem to have it neatly sussed out already.'

'It wasn't difficult. Most of the meal was still un-digested.' A brief pause while the last stitch was made and tied off and the gut cut. 'Death oc-curred—I'd say—within four hours or so of when-ever he finished his last meal. That help?'

Roper did some quick mental arithmetic. The girl from the agency—the maid, waitress, whatever—had left the house at ten-thirty. Dinner had started at eight-thirty, so it had probably finished round about ten o'clock—or even nine-thirty. So Winterton had probably died at some time between one-thirty and two o'clock.

'Indeed it does, sir,' he said. 'Indeed it does. How about rigor?'

'No indicator,' said Wilson, his green mask making him sound terser than he really was. 'Especially in this instance. It was all wrong, y'see. I think it developed inside somewhere—where it was warm, at one rate—and decelerated when the body was put outside. And I can't—I'm sorry—tell you when the body was taken out. So I'd have to *guess* at some median time when the body might have been put outside. Between two and four—a.m.—say. And that ties up with the patches of lividity on the old chap's backside.... Although I couldn't possibly testify to that in court, you understand.'

'How about the cause of death. Any ideas?'

'The cause? That's up to you chaps to sort out. But I *can* detail the injuries that led to his death, not quite the same thing. A head wound. Scalp. Fractured skull, an edge of bone driven into the brain tissues. Not too much splintering of the skull.'

'How about a weapon?'

'I doubt there was such a thing. A weapon as such, that is. The frontal lobes were damaged.'

'Frontal?' said Roper, to whom most medical definitions were so much opaque jargon. 'You mean *at* the front, sir? How come, if the wound was at the back?'

'We call it a *contre coup* injury, in the trade,' said Wilson. 'Means "against the blow". Action and reaction. Think of the brain as a tennis ball in a toffee tin. Bang the bottom of the toffee tin up and down

on the floor and the tennis ball goes up and down
with it. Eventually, the ball starts to bounce in the
tin. Eventually bounces as high as the lid. Brain does
exactly that, except that its not made quite as stur-
dily as a tennis ball. See the point?'

'Graphically, sir,' said Roper. 'So what you're
saying is that somebody banged his head on the
floor, is that it? It couldn't have been an accident?'

'Banged his head on the floor several times, I'd
say, or a wall. Once could have been accidental—
more than once, I'd have said, was a sign of aggra-
vated assault, wouldn't you?'

'So he *was* murdered?'

'Definitely.'

'How about the broken blood vessels up his
nose?'

'At a guess? A punch. An old-fashioned punch on
the nose. But that certainly didn't kill him. Too light
a blow. Arthur,' Wilson broke off to summon the
attendant, 'you can stitch that flap of scalp back,
there's a good chap. I think we've finished up at that
end. Now the insides, Superintendent. They were
adrift here and there. Caused by the fall, no doubt
about that at all. As were the compound fractures of
the right leg—femur cracked in the middle and came
out through the flesh like the point of a knife. But
that was afterwards, between one and two hours afterwards I'd say. Not a great deal of bleeding, you
see. My serologist will be able to tell us more accurately, of course, but that's my guess.'

'So he didn't land on the beach at half-past five
in the morning, did he?'

'Certainly not. Sooner. What's your evidence for
half-past five?'

'Broken wristwatch. That's when it had stopped.'

'Hah! That old dodge,' said Wilson cheerfully. 'If as you say he finished his last meal around ten o'clock last night, then I'd say the poor old fellow's leg was shattered…oh…say…three o'clock…ish. Got any ideas of your own have you, Mr. Roper?'

'A few,' said Roper. 'But not half enough yet. Tell me, sir, there's another body here, a man called Crossways, Saul Crossways. A vagrant, and I think his death and this one are connected. I don't know how and I don't know why, but my gut tells me that if I know the answers to either I'll get a pointer to the other one. Can you manage Crossways today, do you think?'

'Down to the District Coroner, really. But I'll ring him and see if he can get the necessary documents over here. Pronto.' Wilson glanced over to the clock on the wall above the door. 'It's four-thirty now. I was going to give this one another couple of hours but I don't think I'll find any more evidence than I already have. So, say eight o'clock? I'll have Crossways opened up by then and perhaps be able to tell you something. A glimmering, at least.'

'Be obliged, sir. Thanks.'

The mask twitched as Wilson smiled behind it. 'See you at eight then, Superintendent. Perhaps we can have a drink together. Sorry, can't shake hands. Messy. What?'

ROPER DREW THE Fiesta to a stop in front of Vestry's open garage. Light spilled out of it from the battery of portable floodlights. Miller stood just outside it, stamping his feet and blowing on his hands, and Vestry himself, for whom this was one of the most exciting events of his humdrum life, was watching every move with the gleeful interest of a ghoul at a traffic accident.

'Good evening, Superintendent. Cold? Yes?'

'Yes, sir. Bloody cold.'

Vestry had already lost interest in Roper and turned back with hunched shoulders and his hands jammed deeply in his overcoat pockets to watch every move of the technicians, however trivial and however quotidian.

'They found anything?'

'No,' said Miller. He jerked his head towards Vestry. 'And we won't either. He's too happy.'

Vestry's little Peugeot was filthy, covered in grime and splashed with mud. The open garage doors had scraped away the snow in the driveway and left two black arcs. There were only two sets of tyre-tracks, the one from the technicians' van and the other from the Fiesta. If the Peugeot had been anywhere at all, it certainly hadn't been there last night. There was no spreading damp patches under the tyres and the mud in the treads was almost dry.

'How were things at the mortuary?' asked Miller.

'A new bloke. Wilson. Confirmed everything we thought. Somebody laid Winterton out, then chucked the body over the cliff to get rid of it. He's going to check over Crossways too. With any luck, we'll soon have a result.'

'You reckon?'

'I reckon.' Roper looked along his shoulder. 'Have faith, son.'

Miller stayed doubtful and continued to stamp his feet.

Roper took out his cheroots and lit one. Time to

relax. There were moments when even a superintendent could only stand around and do nothing and
this was one of them. He took in the back of the
Peugeot, the two technicians, one dusting the outside, the other going over the inside with tweezers
and a magnifying glass. And then, again, the back
hatch of the Peugeot with its filthy screen and...

And slowly, not so much dawning as surfacing,
perhaps because, unlike Miller, he was a patient man
and didn't mind the chill striking up through the
soles of his shoes and could, for a while, be still, he
suddenly realised what his eyes had earlier seen but
his mind had only just fixed upon.

'Mr. Vestry, sir?'

'Yes.' Vestry trotted over eagerly. 'Yes, Superintendent?'

'Your car, sir. When did you last clean it?'

'Oh, dear, yes,' admitted Vestry, with a contrite
little smile. 'Remiss of me. I'm afraid I don't have
a great deal of time. I usually get the school porter
to hose it down for me—but what with Christmas
and the holidays, it must be four or five weeks. Perhaps more.'

'You're sure, sir?'

'Oh, yes,' said Vestry. 'Indeed yes. Quite sure.
It's been ages.'

'Will you be using the car tonight, sir, or tomorrow?'

No, Vestry was not using his car either tonight or
tomorrow. And, yes, the superintendent could take
it away for a more detailed examination.

'Why? Dare I ask?'

'Just a closer look, sir. And I'll get it polished up

for you. Make some recompense for all the trouble we've been.'

'Why,' beamed Vestry. 'How very considerate of you, Superintendent.'

'Not at all, sir,' said Roper. 'Our pleasure.'

Leaving Vestry still absorbed by the sight of the forensic spring cleaning Roper took the few paces back to Miller.

'The back of that Peugeot,' he said quietly. 'Hatch, frame, windscreen, bumper, over-riders—the whole damned shoot—I want every inch dusted for prints. Then I want every square inch photographed. Close up. Life size. Then I want all the prints stuck together to make one big photograph. Then I want some dust samples—from places where there aren't any prints. And I want those bagged up and analysed.'

'It'll be road dust,' said Miller.

'So it's only road dust,' said Roper. 'But I want it broken down. Microscopic, spectral, analysis—whatever'll stand up in court as gilt-edged evidence. And then I want to know if the dust on that car matches the dust on those old gloves of Coverley's.'

'So you *do* think it was Coverley?'

'Don't know,' said Roper. 'But if it wasn't, I've a damned good idea who it might have been. And when the lads have finished here, I want that car taken back to the station and locked up for the night so that jack-the-lad, whoever he is, can't touch it. And find a couple of volunteers to hose it down and wax it. Like new.'

'But there might be evidence,' said Miller.

'No, lad,' said Roper. 'That's the point. We're not looking for evidence, we're looking for something that *isn't* there. And if it *isn't*, we might even have solved the riddle of the universe. Right?'

SEVENTEEN

THE PATHOLOGIST dropped his plastic gloves into the pedal bin beside the handbasin and began to sluice his hands and forearms under the sprinkler.

'Male. White. Age—approximately—seventy years. Quite well nourished considering the circumstances. Body weight—what *was* the body weight, Arthur?'

'Ten stones thirteen pounds, Mr. Wilson—and fifteen ounces,' piped up the lugubrious youth, soaping his tattoos in the adjacent sink.

'Thank you, Arthur. Eleven stones, less a toe or two.'

'How did he die, sir?'

'Naturally,' said Wilson. 'Massive coronary seizure. Couldn't have taken more than two or three minutes. And if that hadn't killed him his liver and lungs soon would have. Cirrhosis—severe—and over fifty per cent of cancerous tissues in each lung. No general practitioner would have given him more than a year. Sorry. Nobody killed the poor old fellow; he did it all by himself. Meths and thrice-reconstituted dog-ends, no doubt.'

'No, sir,' said Roper.

'Oh, but yes, sir.' Wilson reached for the tongue of paper tissue sticking out of the towel machine on the tiled wall, yanked out a yard of it and ripped it off. 'Sorry, Superintendent. Your Mr. Crossways died of a coronary seizure....'

'And walked a couple of hundred yards afterwards. Up hill.'

'No,' said Wilson curtly, scrubbing the paper over his forearms. 'Impossible.'

'His nose was damaged.'

'So it was. But he certainly didn't die of a superficial nose injury.... I've no doubt that, in the poor fellow's last extremity, he subsided to his knees, then fell forward on to his face. And he wouldn't have walked from anywhere to wherever.... He died where your constable found him. Or he was a member of the Magic Circle. Sorry.'

ROPER BRAKED the white Fiesta at the edge of the cliff road, so that its headlights bathed the warning sign at the base of which Crossways' belongings had been found.

'There, Mr. Wilson. His bag of tat, his cap and his whisky bottle.' Roper was pointing through the windscreen. 'All within a couple of yards of that sign. We think he was trying to broach the whisky bottle—and we know he was there because his dabs were all over the post—fresh ones. Looked as if he'd grabbed at it, then slid down it and finished up on his behind in the snow. And from the state of the snow round about, we also think that somebody might have stopped to help him. Or kill him. Now I'll show you where we found him.'

THE CRYPT WAS DARK and silent and as cold as flint. Two streams of breath vapourised mistily in the beam from Roper's torch.

'His bed—his kettle—and his collection of meths bottles.'

'Blue meths?'

'Mostly.'

'Must have stunk like a tom-cat.'

'He did,' said Roper. The oval of light distorted as it swung across the stone floor to the outline in yellow chalk. 'And that's where the bobby found him.'

Wilson hoisted the hem of his overcoat and sat on his heels on the bottom step and gravely regarded the chalked outline.

'It's odd,' he agreed. 'And interesting. And I *do* see your point.... But he died here. He simply could not have walked from where you showed me to this place. In effect, his lungs would have been slowly filling with mucus and he would have been drowning in the stuff. And since half his lungs were useless in any event, he would have been struggling for breath from the very first step.'

'Supposing he'd been carried? Would you know?'

'Afraid not. Any signs of physical contact, anything in his nailscrapings?'

'Not according to forensic. Just dirt. Mostly his.'

'Pity,' Wilson slowly rose. 'But if he'd been carried, you must have found footprints—somebody else's.'

'A mess of 'em,' said Roper. 'But there'd been another fall of snow. Heavy one.' He stood aside and shone the torch up the steps as Wilson preceded him. The cloudless black sky was pricked with stars and it was almost too cold to breathe without making a conscious effort. They started along the path.

'If he *was* brought here from where you say,' said Wilson, puzzled, 'someone was either ineptly trying to help him...'

'No, sir. They weren't. Whoever it was, they had no intention of helping him.... They wanted him out of the way—and somebody else too, I think.'

Wilson shot an interested sideways glance. 'I do believe you've got it all sewn up, Superintendent.'

'Yes, sir,' said Roper. 'I do believe we have.'

'You promised me a drink. Do I still get it?'

'Drink, sir? I'll buy you doubles.'

IT WAS TEN O'CLOCK and the duty shift were straggling noisily out of the parade room on their way to their respective beats. In the parade room, Miller and a D.C. and the night sergeant were heads together over a local gazetteer open on the table.

'Got those gloves yet?' asked Roper as he turned in through the doorway.

'No, sir,' said the sergeant. 'Harris here, he's on his way now.'

'And he needs a bloody map, does he?'

'D.C. Harris is new,' said Miller, with a hard bite in his voice, '...Sir. Posted here from another division. Today. He doesn't know his way about yet.... Sir.'

'Sorry,' said Roper. And to the uncomfortably embarrassed Harris: 'Sorry, son. But it's getting late and we're all getting bloody tired. You find Mr. Coverley, wherever he is—home, pottery, boozer, wherever—and ask him if you can borrow his driving gloves till tomorrow, the ones Mrs. Fowler bought him for Christmas. And when you've got 'em in your hot little hand, put 'em in a bag, bring 'em back here and get one of the motor-cycle lads to whip 'em over to forensics. There'll be somebody there waiting to shove them under a microscope.'

'But supposing Mr. Coverley won't hand them over, sir; if he wants to see a warrant?'

'Then you charm him, lad. Tell him you're new to the game and you've got a super with stainless-steel teeth. Right?'

'Right,' said Harris.

'Go on, then,' said Roper. 'Hoppit.... If you can manage to get back before you've gone, I'll write you up a commendation. Young Policeman of the Year Award. Go on.'

And, unsure whether to laugh or merely look relieved, Harris hopped it.

AND THEN it was midnight. The dead hour. A solitary D. and D. locked up downstairs. A desk littered with paper cups, and four dead cheroot ends in the glass ashtray and three sheets of A.4 lined paper covered in Roper's sprawling handwriting that, upsidedown, looked like shorthand. Miller had gone home for the night. Somewhere, downstairs, someone was pecking away hesitantly at a typewriter.

Roper stifled a yawn.

A rap on the door was the duty sergeant. He carried two coffees precariously balanced on a plastic tray.

'Thought you'd like another gargle.'

'Thanks,' said Roper. Like himself, the sergeant was an old stager, a copper all the way down to the rubber soles of his boots. He would never make inspector, but he'd see his time out to his pension all the same. He knew it all, had probably pounded a thousand miles of pavement, filled in God alone knew how many Charge Forms, Arrest Forms, Crime Report Forms, Prisoners' Property Forms and

Occurrence Reports, and knew this place backwards, forwards and sideways, and up and down as well.

'You a local man?'

'Yes, sir. Always have been.'

'Your patch then?'

'Right.'

'Married?'

'Yes, sir. Thirty years. Two kids. Got a grand-child, too. Little girl.'

'Well, good on you.' Roper sipped at the new hot coffee. 'Saul Crossways. Did you know him?'

'Old Saul?' The sergeant's face crumpled into something very close to affection. 'Sure. We all knew old Saul. Came here just after the war. I was only a kid myself at the time, and he wasn't so old then either.'

'Take a chair,' said Roper, clearing a space for the sergeant to put the tray down. 'Tell me about him.'

'EX-SOLDIER, Eighth Army. Crossed in love so he told me once—one night when I had to nick him to dry him out.'

'No records,' said Roper. 'I've checked. Here, and at County. No forms at all. And yet you say you nicked him pretty often—on a regular basis you might say.'

'Well, me—or one of the lads. For his own good.'

'No charges then?'

The sergeant looked abashed and went into hiding behind his plastic cup.

'No, sir. We never did. He was harmless, you see. We all had a soft spot for the old bugger.'

'He used to carry a plastic bag.'

'I can remember the old days, when it was only a paper one.'

'Was he ever without it?'

'If he was, I never saw him.'

'How about when he was *really* boozed?'

'Simple,' said the sergeant. 'He tied it round his middle with a piece of washing line. He was never without it. And when the bobby who was keeping an eye down at the cove this morning radioed in to tell me he'd found old Saul dead, my first question was: "How?" And my second one: "Is his bag with him?" Last Christmas twelvemonth, a gang of lads knocked him about for the sheer hell of it. When we took him along to the infirmary he was only a shade short of being unconscious. But he still had a tight hold on that bag.'

AND THEN it was one o'clock and Roper's eyelids were lined with grit and the original three sheets of A.4 notepaper had been consigned to the wastepaper bin and two more, covered in more orderly hand-writing, had replaced them on his blotter. Down the margins the letters Q and A alternated. Only the last three Qs had blank spaces adjacent to the As beneath them.

Unlike the sergeant downstairs, Roper had no one at home waiting for him; although there was a certain middle-aged lady with whom he occasionally shared both board and bed to their mutual satisfaction. When he put in his papers—this year, next year, it wouldn't be too long now—they might make the arrangement more permanent, and open that antique shop. But for now, however late the hour, he was a copper with his teeth into something, and if it was necessary he was prepared to stay awake all night if he had to and worry it to death like a terrier.

He scratched a series of horizontal and vertical lines, like a family tree, a hierarchy of all his doubts and half-doubts and suspicions. G.W.—George Winterton—headed it, the progenitor as it were; and S.C.—Crossways—was labelled down at the bottom as the ultimate issue. He wedded Julian Winterton with Faulkner, Coverley with Julian Winterton, Winterton with Mrs. Fowler, Mrs. Fowler with Glenda Winterton, Faulkner with Glenda Winterton, Hugo Faulkner with Mrs. Fowler...since nothing was impossible. The permutations, at this late hour, seemed infinite. Two. One inside the house, one outside it. There had to be two, paired off in some way, however unlikely....

The telephone rang, sharp, sudden. And so detached and absorbed was he now that it was a moment before he remembered that he was expecting a call.

'Roper. Yes?'

And for very nearly a minute that was all he said. He cupped the receiver closer.

'You're sure? No doubt at all? The gloves and a full report. Here tomorrow. Ten o'clock. a.m.—can you do that?' And already his hand was spidered over the sheet of paper upon which he had been doodling his hierarchy and was tearing it off the pad and crushing it into a ball. 'Bless you, my dear. Bless and thrice bless. —Thank you.'

He let the receiver drop the last half-inch to the rest with a gesture of unmitigated satisfaction, and tossed the crumpled paper ball into the wastepaper bin. The guessing games were over.

Then, from one of the wire trays, he lifted the Xeroxed copy of the handwritten draft that detailed the forensic team's findings about Coverley's Volvo. An hour ago it might have damned Coverley to twenty years. It no longer did.

On an impulse then—and he was rarely given to impulses—he picked up the telephone again.

'Get me the pottery, old son, will you. See if Mr. Coverley's still there.'

'WOULD YOU like a cup of coffee? It's a bit stewed, and I've only got a mug.'

'Thanks,' said Roper, making himself comfortable in Coverley's spare chair.

'Checking up on me, eh?' said Coverley, spooning sugar into a green china mug. He was in a tee-shirt and jeans and still half asleep. Across the office, a campbed with disordered covers and a dented pillow was reasonable evidence that he had indeed been asleep when Roper had rung him.

'No, not exactly,' said Roper. 'Just tying up a few loose ends.'

'Never give up, do you, you people?'

Coverley handed Roper the thick chunky mug on his way by and sat down opposite him.

'Thanks,' said Roper. He sipped at the coffee. 'I'm like you, Mr. Coverley. When the devil drives, I can work twenty-four hours a day.'

'Job satisfaction?'

'Right.'

Coverley slid across a plastic coaster advertising somebody's lager.

Roper carefully set the mug at its centre.

Coverley sat back with both arms along the arms

of his chair. 'I didn't kill 'em, you know,' he said. 'Either of 'em.'

'No, Mr. Coverley,' said Roper. 'I've already worked that out for myself.'

Coverley blew a long sigh of relief. 'Well, I'll be damned,' he said. 'Do you know who did?'

'Perhaps,' said Roper.

'But you didn't turn out in the middle of the night to tell me I'm in the clear.'

'I didn't say you were in the clear, Mr. Coverley. I only said I didn't think you'd killed them.' Roper picked up the mug again and took a long slow sip from it. 'I came about your car. It wasn't clean. Forensically speaking.'

'I don't follow,' said Coverley.

'There were some hairs in it. Grey ones. They match the clippings the path. people took from Saul Crossways. And there was damp on the carpet in front of the back seat. And a muddy heelprint.'

'I haven't used the back seat for days. Before Christmas.'

'Which means somebody else did. Right?'

Coverley didn't answer, nor did he need to. His expression said it all.

'Where was your car last night, Mr. Coverley? Between about half-past ten and midnight. In the yard; in the street outside; in your garage at home?'

'I left it in the street outside. Across the yard gates. It's a way of letting your chaps know I'm in here if they see any lights burning in the works.'

'Sensible,' agreed Roper.

A long silence ensued, the silence that Coverley needed to come to terms with what he knew to be an inarguable truth.

'Perhaps kids borrowed it. For a joy-ride,' he said hopefully.

But Roper was already shaking his head. 'Has she got a set of keys to it, sir?'

'Yes,' said Coverley. 'But it's impossible. Has to be. She couldn't have done it on her own, could she?'

'No, sir,' said Roper. Then he said, with perhaps more sympathy than he had permitted himself all day: 'I'm sorry, Mr. Coverley. But somebody's tried to set you up. Put you in the frame as we say. Twice. The first time might have been inadvertently. But not the second time.'

Coverley stayed silent. He opened the top drawer of his desk and took out a cigarette packet. It was empty. Absently, he tossed it into the wastepaper bin.

Roper pushed his cheroot-case across the desk.

'Thanks,' said Coverley. He lit one with an unsteady hand and shook out the match. 'She must have had an accomplice, mustn't she?'

'Yes, she did.'

'A man, was it?'

'Perhaps,' said Roper, again. He had known about the man after that moment of blinding insight as he had stood behind Vestry's car. It had been Mrs. Fowler who had been the unknown.

'You won't say?' said Coverley.

'I can't,' said Roper. 'More than my job's worth.'

'Yes, of course,' said Coverley. The two of them were no longer adversaries, were even, in a curious way, arriving at something close to friendship.

'When you left your car outside Westwinds house

the other night, was the hatch wired down—or was
the lock working then?'

'It was wired,' said Coverley. He looked momen-
tarily puzzled. 'But that wouldn't have mattered,
surely. She has a key.'

But Roper was already on another track. 'When
you pushed Mr. Vestry's car the other night, who
was on the right-hand side?'

'I was,' said Coverley. 'Faulkner was on the left
and Julian Winterton was in the middle.'

'Has she ever mentioned South Africa to you, Mr.
Coverley? Durban, say?'

Coverley shook his head. She. Her name still as
yet unspoken between them, like the name of God
to the old Jews.

'I knew there was a blank spot,' he said. 'A few
years.... But I didn't push to find out because I knew
in the end she'd tell me. She did about that business
with—what was his name? The M.P.'

'Fanning.'

'Yes. Fanning.'

Another silence. Roper looked at Coverley. Coverley looked at Roper.

'You don't seem surprised, Mr. Coverley,' Roper
said quietly. 'No leaping in the air. No hysterics. If
I'd been you, I'd have gone for my throat and torn
it out.'

Coverley dredged up half a smile. 'Yesterday, I
might have. But I've been putting a few two and
twos together myself. The keys I was supposed to
be the last person to see—the gloves I couldn't find.
Old George—if I think hard, I don't reckon he did
know what I *was* talking about the other night when
I asked him to step into that study. I think he was

as baffled as I was angry. I don't think he knew about Grace and me at all. Not now.'

'Have you told Mrs. Fowler that?'

'Hell, no,' said Coverley. 'I've only connected it all together myself while I've been sitting here talking to you.'

'And will you tell her? As soon as I've gone, perhaps pick up that 'phone and bend her ear a bit? Or not?'

'No, I shan't,' said Coverley. 'As soon as you've gone, I'm going to turn in again and sleep on it. I couldn't even find the words to say to her.... If you're right.'

'She's a clever woman, Mr. Coverley. And to be frank, I don't have any evidence against her, only your word that she's got a set of keys for your car—and if she chooses to deny that, it's only your word against hers. You follow?' Roper twisted out his cheroot in the ashtray. 'I've got to flush her out, Mr. Coverley. Will you help? Keep your mouth shut for a few more hours? I'm not asking you to point the finger exactly, but I'll have to give you some stick and you'll have to play along with me. Will you do that?'

Coverley stretched his mouth into a thin, dubious line for several seconds while he made up his mind. Then his cheroot followed Roper's into the ashtray. 'Yes,' he said. 'I'll help. Whatever you say.'

EIGHTEEN

THE UNEASY COVEN was beginning to gather on the apron of the driveway in front of Westwinds House. Faulkner and his wife had driven in a few minutes ago, Coverley was parking his car and Julian Winterton and his wife had just come out of the house with Mrs. Fowler. It was coming up for mid-day. A chill wind gusted from the direction of the sea and the pale wintry sunshine was doing little to warm it.

Roper and Miller stood apart; and at a discreet distance from them a W.P.C. and a uniformed constable and a sergeant stood in a silent huddle like mourners sombrely waiting for a funeral to start. Further down the drive, two red-banded white Fiestas bearing the County Police insignia lent their further weight to the occasion.

Mrs. Fowler either guessed nothing or was a better actress than Roper supposed. She was chatting to the Faulkners. Glenda Winterton, stamping her elegantly booted foot and shivering dramatically, was clearly muttering her outrage to her husband at having to stand about like this on a cold winter's morning. Coverley, sensibly, after a wave to Mrs. Fowler, stayed in his car and was fiddling deedily with the wires behind his dashboard.

Then, finally, Vestry's little Peugeot came sedately into view between the distant spruce trees. Hosed down, waxed and polished, it was a far cry from the grubby relic it had looked yesterday. Vestry jerked it to a stop beside Roper and Miller and wound down his window.

'I'm sorry I'm late, Superintendent. What would you like me to do?'

'Just park it, sir. As near as you remember to where you left it the other night.'

'Yes. Surely.' Vestry was as gnomishly eager to take part this afternoon as he had been yesterday; and fussily and interminably, and inexpertly, and horrendously crashing through his gearbox—so that the uniformed sergeant had to turn away and Roper distinctly heard him mutter 'Cherist!' to his two colleagues—Vestry jolted the Peugeot backwards and forwards until at last it was placed to his satisfaction between Coverley's Volvo and Faulkner's Rover, both of which he had several times only narrowly missed.

Roper joined him and leaned in at the window. 'This is it, is it, sir? Mr. Coverley's car on this side and Mr. Faulkner's on the other one?'

'Yes,' said Vestry. 'I'm sure. Do you want me to get out?'

'No, sir, stay put. I'll tell you when.'

The coven fell to silence and broke apart as Roper, wearing his Sunday best smile, descended upon it.

He apologised for dragging them all out into the cold. A few minutes, and he and his crew would be on their way again...

'Now I'd like you all to look at Mr. Coverley's car. See where it is, and which way round it is, and its relationship to the house.'

Five pairs of eyes swivelled to take in the scarlet

Volvo. Coverley had climbed out now and was standing beside it.

'Now I'd like to ask if anyone disagrees with the fact that that was where Mr. Coverley's car was parked on New Year's Eve. Anyone?'

No one. A shake of heads.

'And Mr. Vestry's car. Is that in the same place?'

All of them nodded. A grunt came from Coverley. Glenda Winterton rammed her hands deeper into her pockets and hunched her shoulders even closer to her ears.

'You don't seem to agree, Mr. Coverley.'

'I said yes,' muttered Coverley, for a second or two the focus of everyone's attention—as he was fully intended to be. Already on Julian Winterton's face was surfacing a stone-hard interest in Coverley's every shift and utterance. While Mrs. Fowler—'X', last night, on Roper's hierarchy of possibilities, 'X' because even Roper was not averse to clichés when it came to labelling the most obvious unknown in the equation of suspicion—while Mrs. Fowler did her more than passable best to express mounting shock and horror and surprise, and whatever else a woman is supposed to express when her lover is suddenly revealed as a possible murderer. While Coverley, to his credit, or perhaps he really was, looked uncomfortably perplexed.

'Now I want you all to hark back,' said Roper. 'Mr. Vestry tells me that he first left the house the other night at half-past twelve. Who saw him go?'

Glenda Winterton tentatively raised a gloved hand level with her shoulder.

'I did too,' said Mrs. Fowler.

'And I helped him on with his coat,' volunteered

Julian Winterton. 'And I was the one who let him
back into the house again when he couldn't get his
car started.'

Roper was aware of a quickening interest. Even
Glenda Winterton had forgotten how cold it was out
here.

'Then what?' asked Roper.

'Hugo went back out with Mr. Vestry,' piped up
Mrs. Faulkner helpfully. 'I remember that distinctly.
Didn't you, Hugo?'

'That's right,' agreed Faulkner. 'I put on my coat
and went out to the car to see if I could help.'

Vestry had climbed back into the car that night
and opened up the bonnet. Faulkner had tugged
hopefully at a few electrical leads, but had found
nothing obviously amiss.

'Then I got him to try the starter motor. But I
only heard the solenoid click, so I guessed the starter
motor was a bit iffy.'

'You checked the lead to it?'

'It was okay,' said Faulkner. 'Or seemed to be.
And I gave the shaft-end a whack with a spanner in
case the Bendix had seized.'

'But that didn't do the trick either, I take it?'

'No,' agreed Faulkner. 'So I told Vestry to go
back to the house and get some muscle to give him
a push start down the drive here.'

'And who came out?'

'Winterton—Julian, that is, and Coverley.'

'Will you show me how you pushed him? All
three of you. Please.'

Winterton and Faulkner left the coven and joined
Coverley in a line behind the Peugeot. After what
appeared to be a quick rancorous exchange between

Coverley and Julian Winterton the two of them changed places so that Winterton was in the middle.

'And that's where you were all standing, is it? The way you are now?'

They agreed. It was.

Roper ambled across to Vestry.

'I want you to take off your handbrake, sir, and let out your clutch. Now will you all push, gentlemen, please. That's it.'

The Peugeot rolled forward, slowly gathering momentum.

'That'll do,' shouted Roper. 'Nice, gentlemen, thank you. But stay where you are, please. Hands on the car—don't take 'em off.'

Roper moved in behind them. Coverley's hands were on the right-hand side of the door frame of the Peugeot's rear hatch, Faulkner's in an almost identical position on the left and Winterton's hands were splayed just above the bumper in the middle of the hatch.

Roper beckoned to Miller to join him.

'This is not right at all, is it, Inspector?'

'No, sir,' agreed Miller, viewing the three bent backs.

'What's not right,' said Winterton, looking up irritably over his shoulder.

'None of you,' said Roper, casting now for one of the biggest gambles of his working life, 'you're none of you pushing that car from where you were the other night. Right, Inspector?'

'Right, sir,' agreed Miller.

'Now do it right,' said Roper. 'Please get yourselves sorted out, gentlemen.'

Winterton's impatience finally got the better of

him. 'This *is* where we were, for Christ's sake.' He stood upright. 'Coverley was there, Faulkner was there,' he jerked a thumb, 'and I was busting a gut in the middle here.'

'No, sir,' said Roper. 'Definitely not.'

'Look, what's the point?' cut in Faulkner, as he too pushed himself upright. 'And how the hell would *you* know where we were all standing? I mean *we* were doing the bloody pushing, weren't we?'

'Dabs, sir,' said Roper equably. 'Fingerprints. Yours were over there and Mr. Coverley's were over here. Where you are. Big, fat, greasy fingerprints. Both of you.'

'Rubbish,' retorted Faulkner. 'I was wearing…'

A silence fell. Faulkner's jaw clamped shut and the skin on his flabby face went white and tight.

'Wearing what, Mr. Faulkner?'

'Gloves,' blustered Faulkner. 'These gloves.'

'But you didn't have your gloves that night, Mr. Faulkner. You told us that yourself.'

A silence hung, thick and palpable, and Roper let it linger while Faulkner's world slowly crumbled about him.

'Or perhaps you were wearing Mr. Coverley's old gloves? Was that why your fingerprints *weren't* all over the back of Mr. Vestry's car? Eh, Mr. Faulkner?'

'No prints?' Faulkner screwed up his face querulously. His voice rose higher. 'But you said there *were*—you bastards. You said there *were*.'

'I lied, Mr. Faulkner. And now I'm arresting you on suspicion of murdering Mr. George Arnold Winterton…'

'No,' screamed Faulkner, as his hysteria finally broke. 'I didn't! She did! That bitch there! I'm not taking the bloody rap for her!'

And then, pathetically, like a ham actor in a bad play, Faulkner flung up a shaking arm with a trembling finger levelled at the end of it in the classical gesture of exposure.

'You fool,' hissed Grace Fowler. 'You bloody bloody fool.'

ONLY SLOWLY did Faulkner surface from his nightmare. Across the interview room a radiator creaked.

He dragged gratefully on the cigarette that Miller had just passed down to him.

'She rang me.... Grace did. About—oh, I don't know—quarter-past two—something like that, anyway—that's the call I told you about. That kid asking for someone called Daphne. Only it was Grace Fowler.... She told me if I got to Westwinds at once, she had some news for me that would be to my advantage. I told her not to be bloody daft. I thought it was some kind of joke, you see. Then she said, I'd bloody better or the police would get the real story about the fire at the works last year.' Faulkner stared bleakly across at Roper. 'I started that myself. Crazy, but I needed the money off the insurance people, you see. I was half out of my mind with money problems. And it was George himself who put me up to it; he even knew a professional fire raiser...'

'Keep to the point, Mr. Faulkner. First things first, eh?'

Faulkner had gone upstairs to check on his wife. She had fallen asleep, but the telephone ringing had

woken her. But she was drowsy still, and Faulkner
had spun her the story about the girl at the party
asking for Daphne. He had scarcely finished and his
wife was asleep again. Then he had driven hotfoot
to Westwinds.

'Did you use the front door when you got there?'

'No. The back. We'd arranged that over the
'phone.'

At the garden door to the lounge Grace Fowler
had been waiting for him, closing the door and the
curtains as soon as Faulkner stepped inside.

Winterton was dead, she told him. An accident.
Except that the police wouldn't think it was an accident and she needed help. And she really did know
about the fire. His fire, she called it. Your fire. She
could prove it. If she went down for killing Winterton, Faulkner would go down for conspiracy, fraud
and arson. Winterton had told her everything. Everything! She knew everything about everybody in
Winterton's dark little circle of victims.

'And did she?'

'Yes,' said Faulkner. 'She knew more about the
fire than I did. And about old Vestry being a
queer...'

'Where was he, sir? Mr. Winterton?'

Faulkner, brought up short again, blinked. 'Where
was he? Yes. On the floor. In the kitchen. Face
down.'

'There must have been blood.'

'No, there wasn't,' said Faulkner. 'That's just it.
His head was in a plastic bin liner.... She'd Sello-
taped it round his neck. And she was wearing
kitchen gloves—and the floor was wet by the sink.'

At the sight of all this, Faulkner had all but panicked. He had already guessed that what he was looking at was no accident.

'The way she looked, the crazy way she was acting. Like a bloody madwoman. She told me he'd tripped over and caught his head on the corner of the boiler. But it was the plastic bag, you see. That's why I knew it wasn't right. And I think the wet patch on the floor was where she'd been mopping up blood—and that was nowhere near the boiler.'

'Slow down, Mr. Faulkner. What did you do?'

'I didn't want to do anything except get out. She wanted me to put him in the car and get him down to the cliffs. Sling him over—make it look like a proper accident. She reckoned the early morning tide would carry him out. Nobody would ever know.'

She had promised to wipe Faulkner's slate clean too; all that money he still owed Winterton. She had seen a copy of Winterton's will; he had shown it to her. She was his sole legatee—or had thought that she was.

'You're digressing again, Mr. Faulkner,' said Roper.

'Sorry,' said Faulkner. He reached shakily for the cheap aluminium ashtray on the table and drew it closer. 'Anyway—I've got to be straight with you.... The money did it. Winterton was already dead, and I knew damned well she'd killed him. I mean she'd done a lot of people a favour—me included. And no more harm could come to him, could it. Just getting rid of his body seemed like nothing compared with what she'd done.'

'Did you ask her why she wanted to do that? If it *had* been an accident? Why couldn't she have rung for us?'

'Of course I did,' said Faulkner. 'The first question I asked. She told me she'd already stood one drummed-up murder charge and if she had to stand another one she'd probably get sent down; whether she'd done this one or not.'

'How was Winterton dressed?'

Faulkner hauled desperately on the last of his cigarette. 'His dinner suit—and carpet slippers—one was on his foot and the other one was on the floor under the table.'

'When we found him, he was wearing shoes, overcoat, muffler and gloves—and we found his hat further along the beach.'

It had been Mrs. Fowler's idea to dress him up for the inclement outdoors, *and* to put the keys in his pocket *and* to fetch his stick—the one she had bought him for Christmas—from the rack in the study.

'Wait, Mr. Faulkner. You told us that when you'd left the house after dinner the other night, Winterton's keys were still on the table in the hall. You seemed to make a special point of remembering that.'

'Yes,' said Faulkner. 'She told me to.'

'Why?'

'Winterton never went out without his keys. So she said.'

'That isn't what I asked you, Mr. Faulkner,' said Roper. 'Why did Mrs. Fowler tell you to remember that the keys were on the table when you *first left* the house?'

'It was when I went to pick up the body,' said Faulkner, still not answering Roper's question but another one entirely. 'I wasn't going to do it bare-handed—and I remembered I'd still got Coverley's gloves. She snatched them off me and looked inside the cuffs. I didn't know why—at least, I didn't at the time.'

'But you did later on? Right?'

'Yes. She said if the worst came to the worst the police would think Coverley had killed him. That Coverley could have come back to the house—using the keys.'

'And you didn't object to that? Hiving off the blame on to Coverley?'

But by now Faulkner was committed. He slung Winterton's body over his shoulder like a sack and carried it across to the garage. Between himself and Grace Fowler they managed to wedge the body into the close confines of the back seat of the Fiat. It was almost three o'clock.

Leaving the garage door open for her later return, the two of them had then driven down to the cliff road and parked near the old priory. There they had unloaded the body, draped it across Faulkner's shoulders again. Negotiating the wire fence had been tricky; their only torch had been a miniature plastic thing on Mrs. Fowler's key ring. But once over the fence they were home and dry. Down the ragged path. At the cliff edge, Mrs. Fowler had cut the Sellotape that sealed the bin-liner. The liner had gone into her pocket—then Faulkner had grasped Winterton by the armpits and Mrs. Fowler by his ankles. They had heaved him out into space after the third swing.

'The gloves, Mr. Faulkner. Tell us about the gloves.'

As Roper had already guessed, Faulkner had taken them from Coverley's car.

'It was when I was fiddling about under the bonnet of Vestry's car—I needed a spanner to hit his starter-motor shaft with.'

'You didn't have your own toolkit?'

'I did. It was in the car, but the wife had the keys—back in the house. I always give them to her when I'm likely to have a few drinks. I tried Coverley's back hatch on the offchance. It wasn't locked, just a piece of wire round the handle and the bumper. I opened it up, sorted out a spanner, then I spotted the gloves. They looked pretty tatty and they were in the tool-tray so Coverley had obviously chucked them out. I put them on to keep my hands clean.'

'But you were going to put them back?'

'I forgot,' said Faulkner. 'I did put the spanner back—but I'd wired up the hatch again and it was too much bother to open it again. I was going to give them back to Coverley. But then there was the hassle of pushing Vestry's car—and, in the end, I simply forgot about the gloves. I stuffed them into my overcoat pocket and only remembered them again when I got home.'

'And you put them on again to move Winterton's body. And it was you who threw the stick over the cliffs. Yes?'

'Yes.' It was not all that warm in the interview room but Faulkner's forehead and moustache were beaded with perspiration. 'But as I chucked it over, a splinter or something caught the glove.' He looked bleakly at Roper over the table. 'Those bloody gloves. I wish I'd never seen the damned things.'

'Did Mrs. Fowler tell you how Winterton had had this so called accident, Mr. Faulkner?'

'Yes. Sort of. She told me he was getting up from a chair and his feet got tangled up with the legs. He fell over. Caught his head on the boiler.'

'But he was nowhere near the boiler. So you say.'

'That's right,' said Faulkner. 'Nor was the wet patch on the tiles. Old George never died anywhere near the boiler.'

'What happened to the gloves, Mr. Faulkner? Afterwards.'

'She kept them. Told me she'd spirit them back into Coverley's car; she had a set of keys. Coverley let her use it sometimes. I knew that; I'd seen her about town in it.'

'And when you got back home, I suppose your wife was conveniently asleep.'

'Yes,' said Faulkner. 'She rolled over and asked me what the time was. I told her it was ten-past two. She didn't even know I'd been out.'

'While we're on the subject of time—who wound Winterton's wristwatch forward?'

'She did,' said Faulkner. She had slipped it from Winterton's wrist in the kitchen, wound it forward to read five-thirty, then slammed it by its bracelet against the top of the boiler. It had stopped after the one blow.

'Why? What was the point?'

'It was to do with the tide taking him out. She reckoned that between that and the time the wristwatch stopped your people would never know *when* Winterton had died.' Faulkner's mouth twitched gloomily upward at the corners. 'Waste of time though, wasn't it. I told her she was overdoing all the embroidery; but she wouldn't listen.'

Miller handed Faulkner another cigarette and struck a match for him.

'Now Crossways, Mr. Faulkner. Tell us what happened to Crossways.'

CROSSWAYS, as Roper had suspected, had damned himself.

Alarmed at Crossways' outpourings in the Mariners' Arms, Faulkner, on the pretext of going to the washroom, had hurried out to the street and the 'phone booth on the corner of the old Custom House. He had telephoned Grace Fowler.

'What time?'

'Soon after the first bell. About twenty-past ten.'

'But Mrs. Winterton was in all evening. She didn't hear the telephone.'

'No. That's right. The telephones at Westwinds can be switched over to wherever someone happens to be. House, garage, old George's study and Mrs. Fowler's quarters. That's probably why Glenda Winterton didn't hear it ring.'

The possibility of a telephone with switchable extensions was something Roper hadn't considered; but then he remembered the call Glenda Winterton had put through to the garage to summon her husband on New Year's morning. So what Faulkner had just proposed was more than likely. When Grace Fowler had gone upstairs last night she had switched the incoming line to her own telephone.

'Right. You telephoned Mrs. Fowler. What then?'

'I ducked out of the Mariners' at closing time and picked her up in the car—at Westwinds. We talked.

She said we'd have to put Crossways away if we wanted to shut him up. I said we couldn't be sure that he *had* seen anything—but she said we couldn't afford to take the risk that he even might have.'

'And you went along with that, did you, Mr. Faulkner?'

Faulkner raised his head tiredly. 'God help me, yes,' he said. 'I'd got myself in deeply, hadn't I? I was bloody frightened. He was just a tramp—nobody was going to miss him.'

'Really,' said Roper. 'That's what you thought was it? That an old man like him didn't matter?'

'Yes. No. Of course he mattered—but I wasn't thinking right.... I was scared and I went along with her.'

'So you thought it was a good idea to put Crossways out of the way? That *is* what you're saying, isn't it, Mr. Faulkner?'

'At the time.'

'That's murder, Mr. Faulkner. Plain and simple.'

'Yes, I know,' said Faulkner wearily. 'I know.'

'When did you decide to use Coverley's car? Whose idea was that?'

'Hers. It was outside the pottery—across the gates. Half an hour and we could get it back there. And I didn't want to use my own car.'

'And you wanted to implicate Coverley again? Or did she?'

'I didn't. For me it was just a way out. I can't answer for her.'

Faulkner had parked his car in a back street behind the pottery and Mrs. Fowler had picked him up there and driven to the *Argus* works to make a telephone call to Coverley in order to give herself an alibi. She had told Coverley she was ringing from Westwinds House.

'What time?'

'Eleven. It must have been about eleven.'

'Coverley tells us it was quarter-past.'

'Because she made a point of *telling* him it was,' said Faulkner. 'I heard her telling him that she'd rung a few minutes before. And she hadn't. When she put the 'phone down she said it was okay, Coverley had only just come up from his works.'

Quickly then, with Mrs. Fowler again at the wheel of Coverley's Volvo, they had driven out of town along the seafront.

The two of them had waited on a lay-by overlooking the sea, a spot often frequented at night by young lovers in motor cars.

'Time? Can you remember?'

'Yes. I remember exactly. It was ten-past eleven. I looked at my watch. I was scared he might not turn up.'

'But you knew he had to come that way?'

'There wasn't another. Only I thought he might have been too boozed to get there. If he'd stopped off in a shop doorway and fallen asleep I knew we'd never find him. Besides, we had to get Coverley's car back.'

'When did you finally see Crossways?'

'About quarter-past eleven. He was in the middle of the road—wandering all over the place. We talked about running him down.'

'Who did?'

'I did,' said Faulkner. 'It seemed quick—and easy. But Grace said we couldn't be sure we'd killed him even if we did run him down. We'd have to go back and check.... Her idea was to get him in the car and take him to the priory and dispose of him there. It was winter, nobody was likely to find him for weeks unless they were looking for him.

. 'Anyway, we followed him. In the car. He kept stopping, and so did we. Then he stopped by the warning sign between the cove and Burrell's Point. We thought he was throwing up. At least, that's what it looked like. He was hanging on to the post of the sign like grim death. Then he sat down in the snow.

'She slipped the car into gear and we drove up beside him. I got out, then Grace Fowler did....'

'With a torch? Did you have a torch?'

'Yes. She gave it to me. She took it out of Coverley's glove compartment.'

'You saw her do that?'

'Yes. She knew exactly where it was. But then she would have, wouldn't she?'

'What did you do then?'

'I saw he was ill. I mean really ill. His face was going black and he couldn't breathe. It looked like a heart attack. And suddenly I didn't want to go through with it any more. He was dying anyway, I told her; all I wanted to do was to get the hell out of it before anybody saw us.'

'Did Mrs. Fowler think the same?'

'No,' said Faulkner. 'She wouldn't have it. We had to get him to the priory, she said. Out of sight. And the time was knocking on, I knew we couldn't stand there all night arguing the toss. I got him in the back seat of the car and she closed the door on him.'

'What about his bag?'

'Bag?' Faulkner frowned. 'What bag? I didn't see a bag.'

'But you did find a torch. Right?'

'I didn't. She did. She went through his pockets in the crypt. In case he'd written something down somewhere. That's when she found the torch.'

It had been Grace Fowler again who had driven the short distance to the priory, and Faulkner who had carried Crossways' dead body along the path to the crypt.

'You said body. You mean he was dead by then? You know that?'

'I heard him go.' Faulkner shuddered. 'Felt him jerk. I couldn't get rid of him quickly enough. At the bottom of the steps I dropped him—I slipped, you see.' Faulkner paused and looked guiltily across the table. It seemed that he regretted more that he had dropped Crossways' dead body than that he had intended to do ill to it while it was still alive.

'Who turned his doss over?'

Grace Fowler had. She had been obsessed by the thought that Crossways might have written down some kind of record of what he had said he might have seen. Faulkner had kept watch upstairs. At this point it was Fowler who was wearing the gloves.

'Did she have the gloves when she came back to the car? D'you remember?'

'No. I don't think so.'

'How about the torches? Did she bring those back to the car?'

'Only one.'

'Will you testify to that in court, Mr. Faulkner?'

There had really been no need to ask the question.

Faulkner had reached the juncture where he would have agreed to anything.

'What did the pair of you do then?'

'She drove us back to the pottery. We changed cars and I dropped her off at Westwinds.'

'Time?'

'About quarter to twelve. I'm not sure. But I got home at five-to.'

'So that you were nicely tucked up in bed when your wife arrived back from her evening out.'

Faulkner nodded again. 'Yes,' he said. 'Luckily. What happens now?'

'I'd say your luck had run out, Mr. Faulkner.' Roper's chair scraped on the plastic tiles of the floor as he slid it back and slowly stood up. 'The inspector here will formally charge you with being an accessory to George Winterton's murder. He'll caution you; and if you're wise, you'll get your solicitor down here to help you make a statement—roughly what you've already told us.'

'And what about Grace Fowler? If I'm going down, then she's going down with me.'

'Don't fret yourself, Mr. Faulkner,' said Roper. 'If the jury's got any sense, you'll both go down.'

A perturbed Miller followed Roper out to the passage.

'He's lying,' he said. 'Remember what Julian and Glenda Winterton told us? Mrs. Fowler was indoors all that evening. Mrs. Winterton heard the sewing machine going upstairs—and Julian Winterton heard Mrs. Fowler's television go off at half-past eleven—*and* he heard her running a bath.'

'But he didn't say exactly when he heard the water running did he?'

'No,' said Miller. 'But he was pretty precise about the time her telly went off, wasn't he? And according to Faulkner she didn't get home until a quarter of an hour afterwards.'

Roper clamped Miller's shoulder. 'Have faith, my son. You charge him. I'll see to the rest.'

ROPER PUT HIS HEAD around the door of the rest room and crooked a forefinger at its solitary occupant.

'D.C. Harris. The new bloke. Right?'

Harris shot to his feet and did his best to drop his newspaper over his sandwich box. 'Harris, sir. Yes, sir.'

'I'm going to give you another chance to make a name for yourself, D.C. Harris. Get your raincoat on. You're going out.'

'Out where, sir?'

'Westwinds House, my son. A matter of life or death, as they say. I want you to look for something....'

NINETEEN

THE INTERVIEW ROOM was deathly quiet. Roper sipped a too-sweet coffee from a plastic cup. Across the room a shirt-sleeved W.P.C. sat with a pencil poised over a shorthand notepad and another W.P.C. sat by the door. A lorry rumbled by in the street, then it was silent again.

Roper put his plastic cup down and stretched his legs more comfortably under the table.

'You know, Mrs. Fowler, we can stay here all night if we have to. These two ladies are on duty till ten o'clock. And when they sign off there'll be two more signing on to replace them. And I can stay awake for twenty-four hours if I have to. So there's no hurry. You just take your time.'

If she heard, she showed no sign of it. Her fixed, permafrost stare stayed focused somewhere in the middle air beyond the W.P.C. with the shorthand notebook.

Upstairs, Hugo Faulkner was closeted with Tasker, the solicitor and Miller, and hopefully scribbling a statement for all he was worth. Faulkner had been easy game. Against Faulkner there was evidence. Against Mrs. Fowler, to date, there was none; and even Faulkner's testimony against her could be ripped to shreds by a good barrister. What Roper had to have was her own word, and the evidence that he had sent D.C. Harris to find at Westwinds even if he had to upend all the dustbins and lift a few floorboards.

'Money was it, Mrs. Fowler?' Roper enquired. 'Winterton going to change his will again, was he? Now that he'd found out about you and Mr. Coverley?'

The chance shaft met no response.

'Didn't know about Mr. Coverley, did he, Mrs. Fowler? Not until Mr. Coverley told him the other evening. And that upset him, didn't it, Mrs. Fowler? Because I reckon there was more between the two of you than your monthly pay cheque, or if there wasn't then Mr. Winterton thought there was. Right?'

Her eyes swivelled slowly and regarded Roper with something akin to contempt.

'Of course I'm only guessing—and you can always stop me if I get too wide of the mark.... I think when all the guests had gone home and young Mr. and Mrs. Winterton were safely tucked up in bed, you and old Mr. Winterton had a right royal ding-dong—in the kitchen most likely. And perhaps he told you that he was seeing Mr. Tasker today—perhaps with a view to changing his will again. I mean, young Mr. Julian was already creeping back into favour again, wasn't he? Perhaps he threatened to cut you out of his will altogether—and leave it all to Julian. Must have worried you, watching your prospects dwindle like that, eh, Mrs. Fowler?'

Roper's voice had little inflection either one way or the other; but it did have a persistence, like water dripping steadily on to a stone.

'How many times did you bang his head on the

kitchen floor, Mrs. Fowler? Twice? Three times? More?'

'I've no idea what you're talking about.'

'And old Saul Crossways; went to a great deal of trouble there, didn't you, Mrs. Fowler? And some shrewd thinking too; Coverley's gloves, Coverley's car, Coverley's torch. Nearly had Mr. Coverley bang to rights as well, didn't you, Mrs. Fowler? I suppose he'd become dispensable, is that it?'

'I didn't leave the house last night. Ask Glenda Winterton. Ask her husband.'

'No good asking *Julian* Winterton, was it? He was out.'

'He came home about ten-past—quarter-past eleven. Ask him.'

'We already have. He told us he came home at *five*-past eleven.'

'I only said *about..* I didn't look at my watch. It was none of my concern.'

'You must have heard him come in then.'

'I did.'

'Over the noise of your television and sewing machine?'

'Yes.'

'I don't think you did, Mrs. Fowler. I think you're guessing. Mr. Faulkner had told you what time Julian Winterton left the Mariners' Arms and you knew roughly how long it would take him to get home. You could be wrong; ten minutes either way. People who wear watches hardly ever look at the bloody things. I don't, so why should you?'

Across the room the shirt-sleeved W.P.C. had at last started to write.

'What time did your television get switched off?'

'Quarter-past eleven.'

'Precisely?'

She shrugged. 'A few minutes either way. Why should I remember?'

'And I'll bet your sewing machine went off almost a quarter of an hour before that. Almost to the minute.'

'Possibly. But if it did, then that only proves that I was in doesn't it?'

'A quarter of an hour to the *minute*, Mrs. Fowler. Or are you missing the point?'

'Obviously.'

'Time switches, Mrs. Fowler,' said Roper. 'The sort you plug in to a wall socket. Switch your lights on and off when you're out. That sort of gadget.'

'I don't have such a thing. Never have.'

The hands of the clock on the wall above the door crept inexorably on towards four o'clock in the afternoon. D.C. Harris was running it close.

'You can't detain me,' challenged Mrs. Fowler. 'You can't even charge me. You don't have any evidence.'

'Mr. Faulkner's upstairs now writing a statement.'

'It will only be his word against mine.'

'But you knew about his fire, Mrs. Fowler. If I wanted to, I could charge you on the strength of that alone.'

'Hearsay,' she sneered. 'A court wouldn't admit it. You forget, I was once married to a barrister.'

'And he died while you were looking after him, too, didn't he, Mrs. Fowler?'

'I told you all about that. And anyway, that was years ago. Past history.'

Roper hunched forward across the table. 'I think

you're a smart woman, Mrs. Fowler. Smart enough to change history when it suits you. A couple of strokes of the pen, you might say.'

Her eyes narrowed warily. 'Meaning what?'

'Meaning I don't think that cross by Coverley's name was put in Winterton's notebook while Winterton was still alive. Because you wouldn't have dared to invite Coverley into that house. I think Winterton had and then you had to live with it. And after you killed Winterton you put the cross beside Coverley's name to prop up your story that Winterton was blackmailing you and that he hated Coverley's guts. That's right, isn't it, Mrs. Fowler?'

'You can't prove...'

A brisk rap at the door put an end to her protest. 'Come in!'

It was D.C. Harris. A Harris triumphant. Two plastic bags swung from his left hand. He laid them on the table in front of Roper. In each was an electrically operated time switch, a small white plastic box with a rotating dial on the front and three brass prongs on the back.

'Where did you find them, son?'

'We found one in the dustbin, sir. The other one was in a plastic rubbish bag beside it—in an empty cat-food tin. When I asked young Mr. Winterton, he said that he remembered one being plugged in on the landing—it switched a standard lamp on and off—and there was another one that worked the towel rail in the main bathroom. That's when he and Mrs. Winterton first arrived before Christmas. And they aren't there now, sir. Neither of 'em. And the foot pedal of her sewing machine was sticky, sir, as if it had been strapped down with Sellotape.'

Roper tipped the switches out of their bags and on to the table. The dials of each were graduated in fifteen minute intervals. Removable steel pins set the switching times. One was set to go on at ten-thirty, off at ten forty-five, and on again at eleven and off at eleven-fifteen—that would have operated her sewing-machine—and the other to cut off at eleven-thirty, which would have switched off the television. But even more to the point the dials of each had stopped when they had been hastily snatched from their wall sockets, soon after eleven-fifty.

Roper held them out, one in each hand, a few inches from Mrs. Fowler's face, a face that by now was no longer dispassionate.

'Now there's a coincidence, eh, Mrs. Fowler? Both of 'em stopped at ten to twelve. Which is five minutes after Mr. Faulkner tells us he dropped you back at Westwinds. And that's about right, eh, Mrs. Fowler?'

IT WAS LATE and it was cold. Out in the lamplit yard Roper settled himself into the warm car beside D.C. Harris and belted himself in.

Faulkner had talked and Mrs. Fowler was talking, and Miller could see to the paperwork. And tomorrow, belatedly, Roper was going to honour his New Year resolution and spend the day with a book and a bottle and his feet stretched towards a blazing fire.

Meanwhile, silently and stealthily, it had begun to snow again.

HARLEQUIN®

INTRIGUE®

When little Adam Kingsley was taken from his nursery in the Kingsley mansion, the Memphis family used all their power and prestige to punish the kidnapper. They believed the crime was solved and the villain condemned…though the boy was never returned. But now, new evidence comes to light that may reveal the truth about…

The Kingsley Baby

Amanda Stevens is at her best for this powerful trilogy of a sensational crime and the three couples whose love lights the way to the truth. Don't miss:

#453 THE HERO'S SON (February)

#458 THE BROTHER'S WIFE (March)

#462 THE LONG-LOST HEIR (April)

What *really* happened that night in the Kingsley nursery?

The three McCullar brothers once stood strong against the lawlessness on their ranches. Then the events of one fateful night shattered their bond and sent them far from home. But their hearts remained with the ranch—and the women—they left behind. And now all three are coming

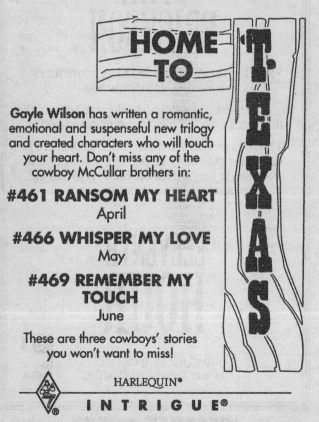

HOME TO

T·E·X·A·S

Gayle Wilson has written a romantic, emotional and suspenseful new trilogy and created characters who will touch your heart. Don't miss any of the cowboy McCullar brothers in:

#461 RANSOM MY HEART
April

#466 WHISPER MY LOVE
May

#469 REMEMBER MY TOUCH
June

These are three cowboys' stories you won't want to miss!

HARLEQUIN®

I N T R I G U E®